P9-DNP-666

Praise for *A Christmas in the Alps*

"*A Christmas in the Alps* by Melody Carlson is the perfect book to get one in the Christmas mood. Second chances, new beginnings, and hope are in full swing in this amazing read."

Urban Lit Magazine

"*A Christmas in the Alps* is old-world charm with a sneaky romance drizzled in that leaves you wanting more!"

Romance Junkies

"A delightful story. Who wouldn't like to look for a treasure in the French Alps at Christmas?"

Evangelical Church Library

Praise for *The Christmas Swap*

"Carlson's latest Christmas romance is as light and sweet as a Hallmark movie."

Booklist

"*The Christmas Swap* is a perfect book to curl up with by the fire and catch some cozy Christmas romance vibes."

Fresh Fiction

A QUILT *for* Christmas

Books by Melody Carlson

Christmas at Harrington's

The Christmas Shoppe

The Joy of Christmas

The Treasure of Christmas

The Christmas Pony

A Simple Christmas Wish

The Christmas Cat

The Christmas Joy Ride

The Christmas Angel Project

The Christmas Blessing

A Christmas by the Sea

Christmas in Winter Hill

The Christmas Swap

A Christmas in the Alps

A Quilt for Christmas

A QUILT for Christmas

A Christmas Novella

MELODY CARLSON

a division of Baker Publishing Group
Grand Rapids, Michigan

Published by Revell
a division of Baker Publishing Group
PO Box 6287, Grand Rapids, MI 49516-6287
www.revellbooks.com

Printed in the United States of America

Library of Congress Cataloging-in-Publication Data
Names: Carlson, Melody, author.
Title: A quilt for Christmas : a Christmas novella / Melody Carlson.
Description: Grand Rapids, MI : Revell, a division of Baker Publishing Group, [2022]
Identifiers: LCCN 2021055319 | ISBN 9780800739348 (cloth) | ISBN 9781493438815 (ebook)
Subjects: LCGFT: Novellas.
Classification: LCC PS3553.A73257 Q55 2022 | DDC 813/.54—dc23/eng/20211118
LC record available at https://lccn.loc.gov/2021055319

Baker Publishing Group publications use paper produced from sustainable forestry practices and post-consumer waste whenever possible.

22 23 24 25 26 27 28 7 6 5 4 3 2 1

CHAPTER ONE

Vera Swanson used to love Christmas. Back in her roomy Craftsman house in Western Oregon, she'd decorate to the nines, then welcome the season as family, friends, and neighbors popped in to admire the holiday décor and partake in homemade goodies. For more than forty years, Vera had played host to homemade storybook Christmases. Oh, they weren't perfect, but what in life was?

Vera's holiday to-do list had always been long and carefully crafted. By Halloween her spare room closet would be neatly stacked with gifts—mostly handmade. And every year on the Friday following Thanksgiving, which she never called Black Friday and never ventured out to a store, Vera would put on her favorite Christmas music and begin decorating her house.

She'd start with the grand oak staircase, artfully wrapping the handrail with evergreen garlands, trimmed with mini pine cones, plaid bows, and white fairy lights. In earlier days she never settled for anything less than aromatic cedar garlands for the stairs project, but as age crept up, along with a weariness of sweeping needle debris from the stairway runner, she switched over to a realistic fake. She'd regularly spritz it with a woodsy pine spray, and no one was the wiser. Her Christmas tree, which had to be real, was put in place exactly two weeks before Christmas. And the next day would find Vera carefully arranging those artfully wrapped gifts beneath it. Picture-perfect.

But Thanksgiving was five days behind her now, and Vera hadn't lifted a finger in holiday preparations. Nor did she intend to. That life was over . . . and there was no turning back the clock. As her father would say, she'd made her bed and now she had to lie in it.

Vera sadly shook her head as she gazed out the window of her condo unit. The view here, even on a clear day, was a bit dreary. Oh, the common grounds had looked promising enough last summer, back when she'd relocated to Eastern Oregon. The leafy trees and grassy areas around the parking lot had seemed almost parklike. But today the browned grass and bare tree branches, draped in freezing fog, seemed to reflect her soul. Bleak and gray and cold.

As Vera turned around to stare blankly at her neatly arranged condo, she knew she had no one to blame but herself. Her son, Bennett, had questioned her abrupt decision to give up the beloved family home and move to Fairview. But after Vera's husband, Larry, passed on, the big old house had grown bigger, emptier, and lonelier with each day. A downsize seemed the only answer, and when a condo unit became available in her daughter, Ginny's, town, Vera had snatched it up. She'd looked forward to being close enough to spend more time with her two grandkids. She imagined attending school functions and keeping them overnight with her. Making cookies and craft projects—playing full-time grandma.

As much as Ginny had wanted her mother nearby, she, too, had questioned the sensibility of giving up the spacious family home that she and Bennett had grown up in. "What will we do for Christmas now?" Ginny asked Vera last summer while helping to sort and pack. "You know how the kids love your house for the holidays. It just won't be the same."

Vera had assured Ginny she was simply passing the torch on to her. "Your lovely home is perfect for family gatherings," she'd said as she insisted Ginny take possession of Vera's plastic bins of treasured Christmas decorations. "I'll even come over to help you decorate."

As it turned out, decorating Ginny's house, or even spending Christmas together, became an impossibility. Ginny's husband's job was transferred to Southern California not long after Vera unpacked her last box. He left immediately, and less than a month later, Ginny and the grandkids followed. Vera vaguely wondered about her Christmas decorations. Had they gone to California too? Or had they wound up in Ginny's castoff pile to be picked up by the Salvation Army?

Then last month, Bennett had called Vera to inform her that he and his new bride would spend the holidays with Lola's family in Montana. He hoped she didn't mind. So Vera would be alone for Christmas—not that she planned to acknowledge the holiday. Who was there to celebrate with anyway? After five months in Fairview, she hadn't made a single friend. She'd heard that as one got older it grew more difficult to make new friends. Perhaps her loneliness was proof of that.

A loud knocking at her door brought Vera's little pity party to a halt. Hurrying to see who was pounding so urgently—since no one ever called on her here—she suddenly remembered she was still in her pajamas and robe. She cracked open the door with a cautious *hello?* but could see no one.

"Please, please, can you help me?" a small voice pleaded from down below.

Vera blinked at the small child who stood on her doorstep. With two messy blond pigtails, bare feet, and widened blue eyes, the little girl looked somewhat lost and confused. And like Vera, the child was dressed in sleepwear, except hers was a thin, summery nightgown that looked none too warm.

"Wh-what?" Vera fumbled to unlatch the chain and fully open the door. "Who *are* you?"

"I'm Fiona," the girl reached for Vera's hand and, grasping it tightly, tugged. "We live right there." She pointed to the opened door across the hallway. "Mama is sick. *Please help me!*"

"Oh my!" Leaving her own door wide open, Vera let the child lead her across the hall and into the condo.

"Mama's in there." The girl pointed to the master bedroom. "She can't get up, and she keeps crying and crying."

"Oh dear." Vera bit her lip. Should she call 911? Find out what was wrong? Or run the opposite direction? "Hello?" she said timidly as she stepped through the door. The only answer was a low groan. "Are you okay?" Vera ventured farther into the dimly lit room. "Your little girl came to—"

"Oh, no, no." A thin woman with dark, matted hair tried to sit up in bed. She waved a hand dismissively. "Fiona should not have—" Her words were cut short as she grabbed her midsection and collapsed backward, gasping in pain.

Vera hurried to the bedside. "Clearly something is wrong. What can I do to help? Should I call someone?"

"No, there's no one . . . nothing. I will be . . . all right." The woman's eyes closed. "A tummy ache. I must've eaten—" She bent over in pain.

Vera leaned over to look more closely at the woman. Her skin was pallid with droplets of perspiration on her forehead. Was she suffering from some kind of flu? What if she was contagious? Or perhaps she had a hangover or drug-related problem. Those things happened. If this was substance abuse, the woman might just need to sleep it off.

Rocking her head from side to side as if to shake off the pain, the woman's knuckles turned white as she gripped the edge of a tattered bedspread. Vera bit her lip. She didn't care if the woman was contagious or suffering from addiction. Something had to be done. "I think you need medical attention," Vera said. "Should I call 911 and request an ambulance?"

"No, please! *Don't* do that." The woman grabbed her hand, holding tightly. "We lost insurance when we moved here. Don't call 911. *Please!*"

Vera glanced back to the doorway where Fiona watched with frightened eyes. The light from the room behind her filtered through the thin nightie making her look slightly ethereal and very small and helpless. "I really believe you should see a doctor," Vera insisted, laying a gentle hand on the woman's shoulder. "Is there someone I can call for you?"

The woman's pale lips drew into a tight line as she opened her eyes. "No, no. We're new here. We have no—" Her words were severed by a gasp.

Vera tried to think. She was new here too, and suddenly more alone than ever. "You need help," she declared. "I'm going to throw on some clothes and then *I* will drive you to Fairview Hospital."

The woman's only response was more moaning. Vera turned to the little girl. "Fiona, can you get yourself dressed and maybe find your mother's coat and some shoes or slippers for her?"

Fiona nodded. "I can do that."

"I'll be right back." Vera hurried back to her condo. Her hands trembled as she awkwardly tugged on her clothes. What was she getting herself into? The woman clearly wanted no medical help. What if she had religious reasons and sued Vera for intruding? But hadn't she mentioned medical insurance—or the lack of it? As Vera shoved her feet into shoes, she wondered what she'd do if the woman refused to go. She couldn't force her. Well, whatever the case, Vera wasn't going to let the poor woman die with her young daughter looking on.

It wasn't easy, but after a shaky trip down the elevator and through the parking lot, supporting the sick woman as best she could, Vera got her and the child into her back seat. She tossed a woolen car blanket over the two, then jumped behind the wheel and, trying to calm herself, started the engine.

Vera navigated the short distance to the hospital, listening to young Fiona's attempts to comfort her mother by saying, "You'll be okay, Mama," again and again. Bless her little heart—what a trouper. The nearby medical facility was one reason the condo location had appealed to Vera. At her age, accessible medical care seemed prudent. But at the moment the short trip seemed to take forever.

Finally, at the ER entrance, help came out and the woman was transported inside. Vera parked her car and helped Fiona out. "Your mother will get good medical attention here. Don't worry, dear, she's in good hands."

"Is she gonna die?" Fiona furrowed her brow. "Like Gramma Albright?"

Vera took Fiona's hand. "No, no, honey. Perhaps it's just—just food poisoning."

"*Poisoning?*" Fiona sounded horrified.

"Not like that. I just meant her stomach might be upset from something she ate. The doctors know how to help her." She squeezed Fiona's cold little hand. "How old are you, anyway?"

"Four." Fiona seemed to walk taller. "I will be five on ninth of January."

Vera tipped her head to one side, studying the child. "You seem to have an accent."

"Accent?" Fiona frowned.

"The way you speak. It's a little different."

Fiona held her chin high. "That's the Irish."

"You're Irish?"

"Yes. Mama is all Irish, but Daddy is all American."

"How interesting."

"I was born in Dublin," Fiona said with pride. "I am Irish American."

"Well, you're a smart girl. You did the right thing to ask

for help today, Fiona. By the way, I don't think I told you my name. I'm Mrs. Swanson."

"Mrs. Swan song?"

"No. Mrs. Swan*son*."

"I like swans," Fiona said. "And I like you."

"I like you too, Fiona." Vera led them into the entrance of the hospital. "Now tell me, what is your last name?"

"Albright. I am Fiona Margaret Albright."

"What a pretty name." Vera remembered seeing kids' stuff in the girl's sparsely furnished condo unit. "Do you have siblings?"

"Huh?" Fiona tilted her head to one side.

"Do you have a brother or sister?"

Fiona nodded vigorously. "I have a big brother and a big sister."

"Where are they now?"

"School."

"Three children. What a nice family. How old are they?"

"Nolan is eleven. Maureen is eight."

As Vera led Fiona toward the reception desk, she calculated the children's age differences—each about three years apart. Perhaps Mrs. Albright was expecting a fourth and simply having morning sickness. But that small condo with three children . . . no insurance. Vera hoped not.

She told the receptionist who they were and then took Fiona to wait in the lobby. After more than an hour of reading the limited children's books to Fiona, Vera went to check with the receptionist. Explaining the situation more plainly, she admitted she barely knew Mrs. Albright and was unsure of what to do next.

"You see, I have Mrs. Albright's youngest child with me, but she has two more children in school. I expect they will be home soon."

The receptionist seemed as uncertain as Vera. "I can't tell you anything about the patient's condition without her consent, except to say it's unlikely she'll be released today. We're still trying to reach her husband. It seems he works out of town during the week."

"I see." Vera felt relieved to hear the man would be contacted. She glanced over to where Fiona was perched on a chair, her feet kicking back and forth. Her expression was a mix of boredom and fear. "Maybe I could leave Mrs. Albright a note, to let her know I'll go home and see to her children while she's here."

"I'm sure that would be a comfort." The receptionist slid a small pad of paper across the desk, then waited as Vera penned a note to Mrs. Albright, including her phone number. "I'll make sure she gets it," the receptionist assured her. But as Vera led Fiona out of the hospital, she felt uneasy . . . and a bit like a kidnapper.

CHAPTER TWO

Neither of them spoke as Vera drove Fiona back to the condominium. It wasn't until they were riding upstairs in the elevator that Vera realized she'd locked the Albright unit when they'd left earlier. "I guess you'll have to stay with me for a bit," she told Fiona as she unlocked her own door.

"That's okay." Fiona walked right in, pausing in the center of the room to look around. "Your *flat* is really pretty."

"My flat?" Vera asked before remembering flat was another word for apartment or condo. She thanked her, glancing around too. Her condo unit was identical to Fiona's. Except, she remembered, the Albrights' unit had seemed rather stark with very little furniture. Naturally Vera's home, with its fixtures, accents, and art, might seem attractive in comparison. Vera had been an interior designer for more than twenty years. She'd carefully chosen her favorite furnishings and artifacts from her previous home, drawing a to-scale plan for where each item would go since space was at a premium here. Then, as she'd artfully arranged everything, she convinced herself that one could be at home anywhere, no matter the square footage. And, really, it wasn't a bad-looking home. Just lonely.

"Are you hungry?" she asked Fiona.

An eager nod motivated Vera to head to the kitchen. She opened the orderly pantry, looking through the shelves for the types of things her grandkids liked. Becca and Benji were a bit older than Fiona, but kids were kids. "Do you like peanut butter and jelly?" she asked.

"Yes!" Fiona answered with enthusiasm. "That's my favorite."

Relieved this girl was easy to please, Vera prepared a plate for her, adding some carrot sticks and apple slices to the dish and pouring a glass of milk. Then, realizing she was hungry too, she prepared an identical plate for herself. When was the last time she had peanut butter and jelly?

After their kid-friendly lunch, Vera pointed Fiona to the hall bathroom where she could wash her sticky hands. When the task took longer than necessary, Vera went to check on the small child and found her in the master bedroom, staring at the bed.

"Hello?" Vera went over to her. "Something of interest here?"

"This is *so* beautiful." Fiona ran a hand over the handmade quilt, an old-fashioned design of varying shades of blue.

"Why, thank you." Vera peeked at Fiona's fingers to reassure herself that they were jelly-free. "I made it myself."

Fiona turned to her with wide-eyed wonder. "*You* made it? All by yourself?"

Vera smiled. "Mostly. Although I did have some friends help me quilt the top. That was back in the day when we did it by hand. This one's called Nordic Star."

"Nordic Star?" Fiona's eyes looked puzzled. "What kind of star is that?"

"Nordic means north like Scandinavia. This is a Scandinavian design. My husband's family was Norwegian."

Fiona slowly nodded as if she understood all about Scandinavia and Norway, but Vera suspected it had gone right over the small girl's head. And then she let out a long deep sigh. "Mama *loves* patchwork quilts."

Vera was impressed that Fiona actually called it a *patchwork* quilt. "She does?"

"Yes." Fiona's eyes lit up. "She has this great big book all full of patchwork quilts. She lets me look at it with her. The quilts are so pretty."

"That sounds like a good book." Vera wondered if she might have the same one in her collection.

"I wish I could make Mama a quilt." Fiona released a smaller sigh. "Just like this one."

Vera smiled. "Maybe someday you can . . . when you're older and learn how to sew." She gently led Fiona out of the bedroom.

"How old do I have to be to sew?"

"Well, you're probably old enough to do some sewing. But a big quilt like mine takes a lot of work. And it's a particularly difficult pattern."

Fiona paused to peer in the spare bedroom, which doubled as a craft and sewing room, not that it had seen much use lately. "Whose room is this?"

"Oh, it's just a place to make things, or have a house-guest." Although she wasn't doing much of either these days. Fiona skipped inside and Vera followed.

"Is this where you made your patchwork quilt?" Fiona asked.

"No, no, I made that quilt a long, long time ago. It was for my husband. Blue was his favorite color." Vera felt a small stab of guilt to remember how she'd been reluctant to use the beautiful quilt for so many years. Worried it would be ruined, she kept it safe in a closet for decades. It wasn't until Larry got sick that she got it out and laid it on their bed. But, oh, how he'd loved it. She remembered how he'd trace the star designs with his fingers, a faraway look in his eyes.

Fiona knelt next to an oversized shaker basket filled with neatly rolled up quilt scraps tied with raffia. Pieces Vera had held on to, not because she planned to use them, but because they looked so pretty, like a fabric rainbow in a basket. "Where's your husband?" Fiona fingered a purple calico print.

Vera forced a smile. "In heaven. He doesn't need the Nordic Star quilt anymore." She sighed. "But I still do."

"Oh?" Fiona turned to her with a creased brow. "Does that mean he died? Just like Gramma Albright?"

"That's right."

Fiona's blue eyes glistened. "Will Mama die too?"

"No, no. She'll be just fine." Vera hoped she wasn't lying. "That's a very good hospital."

"Can you make a quilt for Mama?" Fiona asked eagerly.

"I—uh—I don't know."

"She wants one so bad." Fiona's eyes brightened with

hope. "I can help you make it. We'll make a quilt for Mama to make her better."

Vera didn't know what to say, but hoping to distract Fiona from thoughts of death and sickness, she slowly nodded. "I might be able to quilt your mother *something*." She imagined a small project . . . something that would distract from feeling sorry for herself during the holidays. "Maybe a pillow. Or even a small lap quilt." She held her hands a couple of feet apart. "You know, like this."

"No, Mama needs a big patchwork quilt," Fiona insisted. "For her big bed. Can you do it, Mrs. Swanson? *Please—please!* Mama would be so happy. I promise to help."

Vera didn't know what to say.

"And we will give it to her for Christmas," the precocious child continued.

Vera blinked. A big quilt? By Christmas? Now that would take a miracle.

With her little hands clasped in front of her, Fiona's face bore the most pleading expression Vera had ever witnessed. "Oh, please, please, can we make her one? *Please?*"

"I, uh, I'm not sure. But I promise I'll think about it." Seeking another distraction, Vera checked her watch. "Do you know what time your sister and brother get home from school? I've seen a bus out in front in the morning. Is that for them?"

"Yes. They ride the school bus. When Mama says it's three o'clock that means Nolan and Maureen are almost home. But I can't tell time."

"Well, it's nearly three now." Vera looked out the window into the parking lot. "Does the bus stop down there after school?"

"Yeah. Mama and I used to go down there and wait, but Nolan and Maureen get to ride up the elevator all by themselves now. I never get to do that." She stuck out a pouty lip. "Mama says I'm too little."

"Well, let's leave my door open, Fiona. Your job is to keep watch for them. Let me know when they get here. Since your house is locked up, they'll need to come in here . . ."

"Nolan has his own flat key," Fiona informed her. "Because he's *big*."

"Oh?" Vera didn't think an eleven-year-old was *that* big, but she was relieved the children would have a way to get into their own home.

"Where is your daddy, Fiona? The lady at the hospital said they were trying to reach him."

Fiona frowned. "I don't know. Someplace far away."

Vera considered this. "Does he live somewhere else?"

"Just when he's working. Then he comes home."

"Will he be home today?"

"Nope." Fiona firmly shook her head. "Just weekends."

Vera wasn't sure what to make of that. "Well, you watch for Nolan and Maureen while I clean up our lunch things."

"Okay." Fiona sat on the bench next to the front door, her short legs kicking in and out, and staring into the hallway like a loyal watchdog. Vera's heart twisted at the sight. Such a small child, but so full of love for her mother and her family—and so smart for her age. But youngest children were often like that. As Vera returned to the kitchen, she pondered over the struggling Albright family. A mother in the hospital, a father who seemed to be working far from home, and three children . . . and only a few weeks until Christmas. It all sounded so dismal.

Vera knew a patchwork quilt wouldn't be the answer to the family's problems, but what if she could make Mrs. Albright a quilt by Christmas? What a sweet, unexpected surprise that would be for the young mother. Perhaps the forging of a lasting friendship. Vera shook her head as she put the last plate in the dishwasher and closed the door. Yes, it was a nice idea, but it was impossible.

Vera was only one woman—and not a young energetic one either. A Nordic Star quilt was complicated. It would take a team of three or four women to measure and mark and cut and sew and iron . . . and Vera didn't know a single quilter in this town. In fact, it seemed that her small next-door neighbor was her first actual connection. Not that she didn't appreciate young Fiona Albright's companionship. The child was definitely intelligent and quite thoughtful too. How many almost-five-year-olds wanted to make their mother a patchwork quilt? But Fiona was far too young to be much help in creating a quilt. Really, it was a ridiculous idea.

CHAPTER THREE

After some quick introductions and a brief explanation about their mother, Vera followed the Albright children over to their unit, waiting as Nolan importantly unlocked the door. "Would you like to come in?" he politely asked Vera.

She nodded. "Thank you. We can sort things out."

"Is Mama gonna be all right?" Maureen asked with a furrowed brow. Unlike fair-haired Fiona and Nolan, Maureen definitely resembled her mother with her brunette hair curling loosely over her shoulders and dark brown eyes. Eyes that looked very worried.

"I left my phone number at the hospital," Vera told her. "I hope to hear from them soon."

"Can you ring them?" Nolan said with concern.

"Yes. But how about if we wait a bit?" She patted his messy blond head, wondering when it had last been combed. "Has your mother been sick for long?"

Maureen shrugged. "She felt poorly last night."

"And this morning too," Nolan added. "She didn't make our lunches."

"You haven't eaten?" Vera asked.

"Mama gave us money for school lunch today," Maureen said.

"School lunches are brutal." Nolan frowned.

Vera nodded with sympathy. Maureen's and Nolan's accents were even more distinct than Fiona's.

"Do you know how to reach your dad?" Vera asked Nolan.

"His number is on Mama's phone."

"Where does she keep it?"

"By her bed or in her purse," Maureen said.

After a quick hunt, Nolan located the phone, which was dead. But Maureen found a long cord, and after it was plugged in, Nolan took charge by calling his father. Relieved to hear he'd connected with someone, Vera listened as Nolan quickly explained about their mother being sick and in hospital.

"The neighbor helped out. She's with us now." Nolan waited. "Yeah, she's kind of old. Yeah, like Gramma Albright." He held the phone to Vera. "Dad wants to talk to you, Mrs. Swanson."

She took the phone. "Hello?"

"I'm Josh Albright." The voice on the other end sounded somewhat flustered. "Nolan tells me you've been helping out."

"Yes. I'm Vera Swanson. I took your wife to the hospital around eleven this morning. I really don't know much more, but I believe they were trying to reach you."

"Yes. I only just saw that they'd called about a few hours ago. My construction site is so noisy I didn't hear my phone ring. When I called the hospital to see what was going on, a nurse told me Kerry's appendix had to be removed. She was still in surgery when I called."

"Oh my! I'm glad we got her there."

"Yes. Thank you so much. Kerry had mentioned a stomachache on Sunday before I left to come back up here. I had no idea it was serious."

"Apparently she didn't either."

"The nurse said she'll probably be in the hospital for another day or even two . . ."

Vera didn't know what to say.

"We don't have any family or anyone there in Fairview," Josh continued. "We moved to the US a couple years ago. I wanted to be near my mom since she'd been having some health problems. We were in Ireland before that. That's where I met Kerry. Anyway, we were staying at my mom's . . . but then she passed on."

Vera's heart went out to the man. "I'm sorry."

"Thanks." He blew out a breath. "So I brought my family up here after my mom died. I'd heard there was lots of construction going on in Oregon. But the only decent job I could find was four hours away—working on a big resort hotel. Kerry said take it, so I did. But now I can only come home on weekends. And not every weekend either. Gas costs too much."

"I see." Vera thought for a moment. "And today is only Tuesday so I assume you weren't planning a trip home."

"I was just home last weekend. And I really need the hours at work. We're pretty strapped. To lose three days would be—"

"I suppose I could keep an eye on your children for you. Until your wife gets out of the hospital, that is." She glanced at the three sets of eyes tightly fastened on her.

"I appreciate your offer, but it's too much to ask." He let out a loud sigh. "I should probably just come home today. If I quit at five, I can be there before ten. If you could just mind them until—"

"No, no. You stay there with your work." Vera forced a confident smile for the children's sake. "I'm a grandmother, Mr. Albright. My two grandkids are a little younger than Nolan and Maureen. If you trust me to take care of your kids until your wife can come home, I'm willing to do it."

"This is such a pickle. I don't even know what to say, Mrs. Swanson."

"First off, call me Vera."

"Right. I do appreciate your offer, Vera, but I'm worried what Kerry might say. She's very protective of the kids."

"I understand completely. And although I met your wife briefly, it's not as if you really know me. I can appreciate your hesitation about leaving your kids with a stranger." She pursed her lips to think. "I could give you my son's and daughter's phone numbers if you like. Sort of like references."

"How about if you let me talk to Nolan again?" he said.

"Of course." She handed the phone to Nolan and walked over to the window. She busied herself looking outside and tried not to eavesdrop as Nolan answered questions from his dad that were obviously in reference to her. She was impressed with the boy's surprisingly mature answers and astute observations. Next Nolan handed the phone to Maureen.

"She seems like a nice lady, Daddy. Fiona's been with her a lot today." Maureen answered a few questions then held the phone out to her sister. "Daddy wants to talk to you."

Fiona greeted her dad with enthusiasm. "Mrs. Swanson is really nice, and her flat is really pretty," she chirped into the phone. "And she makes *patchwork* quilts, Daddy! And we're gonna make one for Mama for Christmas." She listened for a bit then passed Vera the phone.

"Well, you seem to have the seal of approval from my kids," Josh told her. "I know it's too much to ask, but if you really don't mind, it would help us out a lot if you could take care of them. Just until Kerry comes home. Hopefully tomorrow."

"I'm pleased to help you," she told him. "I've been hoping to get to know my neighbors, and it seems God set this opportunity quite literally on my doorstep. So really, Josh, I'm more than happy to do this. And I must commend you on your well-mannered children."

He laughed. "Sometimes they are good. How about you let me talk to them again just to make sure they stay on their best behavior?"

First she gave Josh her number then turned the phone back over to Nolan. As each of the kids took turns talking to their dad, Vera looked around. Although the space was disheveled, it wasn't dirty. Just cluttered with the things of the family. And the sparse furnishings consisted of patio furniture and the sort of castoffs one might find at a garage sale or by the side of the road with a FREE sign.

After the children finished talking to their dad and the phone was set aside, Vera cleared her throat and made an announcement. "Well, it seems that you three will be in my care until your mother can come home." She looked at each of them in turn. "I think we will have our meals at my house since I'm more comfortable in my own kitchen, but you kids will sleep in your own beds since all your clothes and things are here. I'll stay overnight here so you won't be alone."

"In Mama's bed?" Fiona asked with interest.

Vera thought of her own luxuriously comfortable Sleep Number bed. "Yes, but I'll bring over my own bedding." She looked at Nolan and Maureen. "If you're anything like my own children used to be, I'll bet you'd like an after-school snack." They both nodded eagerly, and she led them back over to her unit. As she headed for the kitchen, Vera asked Fiona to point her siblings toward the powder room to wash their hands.

"Please, Mrs. Swanson, can I show them *all* of your flat?" Fiona asked politely. "It's so beautiful."

"Of course." Vera opened her fridge with a chuckle. Fiona was four going on forty. While she sliced cheese to melt on crackers, she could hear Fiona giving the full tour of her condo. From the sounds of it, they were in the master bedroom now. "And Mrs. Swanson is going to help me make Mama a big quilt just like this one," Fiona was boasting. "It's called the North Star. But instead of blue, Mama's quilt will be Christmassy colors. Because it's gonna be a *Christmas quilt*."

Nolan and Maureen sounded impressed, but Vera felt concerned as she removed the tray of cheesy crackers from her toaster oven. A big Christmas quilt—*really?* Well, Fiona certainly had an imagination. And she did love her mother.

Christmas is around the corner. Making a big quilt like that isn't a task I could tackle alone."

"We could help you," he said.

She smiled. "I'm sure you could, but you have school and other responsibilities at home. And I'm new in Fairview, so I don't really know anyone I can ask to help—"

"But if you had some help, you *could* make the quilt?" he asked eagerly.

"Yes, I suppose so."

His brow creased as if he was thinking hard. "Gramma Albright had five kittens to give away. You know what we did?"

Vera shook her head with amusement.

"Dad and me made these posters with pictures of the kittens, you know, on the top part. On the bottom part we put our phone number on strips to tear off."

"Oh, yes, I've seen posters like that." She tilted her head to one side, curious as to his point.

"We put posters in shops and at church and stuff. And we got so many phone calls that Gramma said she could've given away dozens of kittens."

"So your poster worked."

"We could do that for you, Mrs. Swanson. We'll make a quilt poster with a picture of your blue quilt on the top. We'll ask for people to come help make a quilt. Ya think that'd work?" His blue eyes looked so intense and hopeful, all she could do was nod.

"It might work," she said, conceding.

"I'll get up early and make the poster on Dad's computer. I know how to work the printer and everything."

"Well, if you want to do that, I don't see that it could hurt.

But keep in mind it's close to Christmas. People might be too busy to give up time to make a quilt."

"Maybe they'd want to," he said. "Some people like to help."

"You're right. People might like to help." She ruffled her fingers through his wavy blond hair. "Now off to bed with you."

* * *

To Vera's amazement, while she was fixing the kids breakfast, Nolan not only conversed with his mother in the hospital but managed to get a pretty good photo of Vera's quilt and print off several posters for her. She read the capitalized words beneath the colored photo with amusement.

WANTED:
PEOPLE WHO WANT TO MAKE A CHRISTMAS QUILT.
PLEASE CALL THE PHONE NUMBER BELOW.

Nolan pointed to the blank area at the bottom of the flyer. "All you need now is to pen your phone number sideways and then cut little strips with shears." He moved his hand like scissors to explain.

"Thank you, I've seen those before. I can do that."

"You'll put the posters up today?"

"Uh, yes, if I have time." She didn't want to be deceitful, but she also didn't care to go around hanging these posters all over town. Besides embarrassing, it would take up a lot of time.

Satisfied that Vera planned to utilize his posters, Nolan

sat down to breakfast with his sisters. He told the girls about talking to their mother and that she might not get to come home until Thursday. Soon it was time for Nolan and Maureen to catch the school bus. Seeing the pair were safely aboard, Fiona and Vera went to work clearing up the breakfast things.

"I know where you can put the quilt posters," Fiona told Vera as she attempted to wipe off the sticky breakfast bar with a paper towel. "We don't even need a car."

"Where's that?" Vera handed Fiona a damp dishrag to replace the paper towel.

"Nick's Market. That's where Mama and I go to get milk and bread and stuff. And there's a pretty flower shop there too. Mama and I look in the window sometimes, but we don't have enough money to buy flowers."

"Oh, I know what you mean. Susan's Flowers. I've been there a few times. But I've never been to Nick's Market," Vera said.

"And there's the big church across the street. We go there sometimes. It's different than our old church, but I like it. And I get to be in the Christmas play."

"That's nice." Vera had noticed the church before. She'd even considered paying it a visit . . . except that she was not ready for that yet. Since losing Larry, she'd been uncertain about church . . . and perhaps even uncertain about God.

"That's three places for us to go." Fiona proudly held up three fingers.

"You're right." Vera nodded with resolve. Best to just get this over with. "Ready to go put up some posters?"

Before long, they were outside, walking through the freezing morning air, with Fiona happily chattering about this and that and everything. Vera had questioned the warmth of Fiona's lightweight jacket, but Fiona seemed to think it was just fine. Even so, Vera wrapped a warm scarf around the little girl's head and neck and wished she had some pint-sized mittens for her. As they walked, Vera tried to appear enthusiastic about the quilt posters, but mostly she felt self-conscious. Surely, the shop owners would think she was nutty. And the church—when she wasn't even a member?

Well, for Fiona's sake—and Nolan's—she would just do it. But after they were finished, she planned to be done with this whole crazy plan. Somehow she'd convince Fiona that a lap quilt would be just the thing. And she'd even let Fiona choose the colors and fabrics and not complain if they looked gaudy or mismatched.

CHAPTER FIVE

Tasha Ellison wasn't a fan of cold weather. She could blame it on her father who'd come from Jamaica as a small boy with his family, nearly fifty years ago. But he'd been entirely absent from her life, so it wasn't like she knew anything about him. Still, she felt certain this longing for warm climates was somehow woven into her DNA. Especially when it was freezing outside like today. To add to Tasha's morning angst, her aunt Susan's order of flowers hadn't arrived and the shop was pretty bare of blooms, leaving Tasha with nothing to arrange. Not that any customers had been by to notice.

Normally Tasha enjoyed working in her aunt's florist shop. Even in the middle of summer with no AC, Tasha never complained about the sweltering, humid heat in here. And although the smell of overly ripe flowers made her mom nauseous, it had a strange appeal to Tasha. Yes, she was pretty much at home in the flower shop. Just not so much in winter.

The tinkling of the bell warned her that a customer had

entered. Hopefully they wouldn't want something to carry with them. If they did, maybe she could convince them that carnations, lilies, and ferns would make a nice bouquet. Because that was about all she had to choose from.

"Hello?" a little girl's voice trilled toward her, and Tasha looked over to see an attractive silver-haired woman and a small child.

"Hello, can I help you, ladies?" Tasha went over to them.

"We have a poster," the little girl proclaimed, holding up a homemade flyer.

"Oh? Well, it's probably good you're not here for flowers. Our delivery truck is late today."

"Can we put this in your shop?" the girl asked.

"Let's see." Tasha took the paper and looked at the photo of a beautiful blue quilt. "How pretty." She paused to read the words. "You want people to help sew a quilt?" She looked from the girl to the woman, who seemed a bit embarrassed but nodded.

"It's for my mama," the girl said, "for Christmas. She's in hospital now and she always wanted a quilt." She tapped the picture on the page. "Mrs. Swanson made this one, but Mama's will be Christmassy."

"Are you Mrs. Swanson?" Tasha asked the woman.

"That's right. I've been quilting for decades."

"You made this?"

"Yes. That one and dozens of others."

"So if I came to help, would you teach me how to sew a quilt like this?"

The woman looked surprised. "Yes, if you wanted. Helping to make a quilt is a wonderful way to learn."

"And are these lessons free?" Tasha asked cautiously.

"Yes, of course. You'd learn to quilt in exchange for your help."

Tasha tore off a phone number. "Then count me in."

"Really?" Mrs. Swanson blinked.

"Absolutely. I'm Tasha Ellison. My aunt owns this shop. I just work mornings and weekends, so I have loads of spare time. And I love working with colors and textiles and have always wanted to learn how to quilt."

Mrs. Swanson stuck out her hand. "I'm very pleased to meet you, Tasha. I'm Vera. I'd love to have your help."

"So how many people are in your quilting group?" Tasha asked.

"Right now, just two, counting you." Vera grinned. "Three, if you count Fiona here. She wants to help too."

Tasha laughed. "How many do you hope to get?"

Vera seemed to think for a moment before answering. "Well, if we had four adults, counting me, I think we could get a quilt done by Christmas. If all goes well."

"Then you're halfway there." Tasha studied the photo more closely. It really did look like a beautifully made quilt. "Let me know when you want to get started and I'll be there with bells on."

Tasha put Vera's number into her phone and added her address while she was at it. They shook hands again then Vera thanked Tasha once more before taking the little girl by the hand. They walked around the little flower shop, pausing to admire this and that before turning back to Tasha, who was taping the sign to the door. "I'd love to get a bouquet for Fiona's mother, for when she comes home from the hospital, but your flower selection does seem a bit limited. Still, maybe you could put—"

"No." Tasha held up a hand. "You really should wait until our delivery gets here. I mean, if you want something really pretty."

"Yes, you're probably right." Vera thanked her one last time, and then they left.

***

Vera still felt slightly stunned as she and Fiona headed for Nick's Market. Tasha seemed like such a sweet girl, so interested and creative too. Her enthusiasm had felt almost contagious, especially, it seemed, to Fiona who practically danced down the sidewalk. "Tasha is really pretty, isn't she, Mrs. Swanson?"

"Yes," Vera agreed. "She's a very beautiful girl."

"I like her. I bet she'll be good at quilt making too."

"She certainly seems eager to learn." Vera paused outside of Nick's Market. It was one of those little neighborhood stores that she normally didn't frequent. The burly guy at the counter looked a little gruff with his torn T-shirt and numerous tattoos, but his smile was friendly as she and Fiona approached him. Before Vera could open her mouth, Fiona was explaining the whole thing—and not doing a bad job of it either.

"Mama's in hospital now," Fiona continued boldly, "but the quilt we're gonna make will be for Christmas, so we have lots of time to sew it. I mean, if we get some help. We really need help."

"Uh-huh." He looked slightly amused.

"Do you mind if we put this flyer up here?" Vera pointed to a crowded bulletin board.

"Sure, help yourself. Everybody else does." He turned his attention to a customer waiting to pay for a carton of beer.

"Excuse me." A well-dressed woman who appeared to be about Vera's age approached with a bottle of orange juice in hand. "Did I hear you correctly? You're looking for someone to help you sew a quilt?"

Fiona thrust a poster in front of the woman. "See the quilt Mrs. Swanson sewed? We want to make one just like that. Only different colors. For my mama. For Christmas."

The woman took the poster from Fiona, studying it closely. "You're handing out posters to find quilters?" She frowned in a way that suggested she disapproved.

"Yes, it's rather unorthodox." Vera started to explain about the Albright children but was interrupted.

"You're an experienced quilter?" The woman peered at Vera through her horn-rimmed glasses. "Are you very good at it?"

"Well, I like to think so. I've been at it for a couple of decades."

"Then why are you looking for people to help you? Don't you have quilter friends?"

Vera quickly explained that she was new in town and didn't know anyone and how the children came up with this idea. "I've made many quilts, but not a large intricate one in such a short amount of time. Not all by myself."

The woman's scrutinizing gaze traveled from Fiona to Vera. "Well, I recently retired from my practice as a licensed therapist. So naturally I have more free time on my hands.

And I have been seeking some sort of hobby to occupy myself."

"Are you interested in quilting?" Vera studied the woman. She didn't seem like the quilter type—was there a type?

"Well, I used to be a fairly good seamstress. Of course, that was eons ago. But I've never attempted a quilt before."

"Would you like to learn?" Vera asked. "It's kind of interesting."

"I think I should give it a try." She stuck out her hand. "I'm Eleanor Rasmussen. I live in Tall Oaks. That's a few blocks from here."

Vera introduced herself, as well as Fiona. The two women exchanged phone numbers and Vera promised to call within the week. Then Vera hung her quilt poster on the crowded board and she and Fiona left. But once they were outside, Vera slowly shook her head. "I can't believe we've already found *two* women interested in quilting," she said to Fiona.

"I can believe it," Fiona said as they waited to cross the street. "Making beautiful quilts will be fun."

"Maybe, but it'll be work too." Vera nodded toward the church. "This will be the last poster we put up for today, Fiona. We need to go home and do some housework."

"Housework?"

"Yes. Don't you want your home to look all fresh and pretty for your mother when she gets out of the hospital?"

"Like your flat?" Fiona's eyes lit up.

"Well, uh, maybe." Vera wasn't so sure about that, but perhaps they could perk it up some.

Vera tried the front door of the church, thinking it might be locked, but it opened. Fiona marched right into the foyer and pointed to a pair of double doors. "That's where the big people go to church. I go down the stairs to my class."

"Sounds like you know your way around here." Vera looked down a hallway that had a sign with an arrow pointing toward OFFICES.

"We used to go to Saint Peter's," Fiona said as Vera led her down the dimly lit hallway. "It's really big. But Mama says it's too far away."

"There's the office." Vera nodded toward the reception area, then lowered her voice. "I'll ask if we can hang our poster, Fiona, but don't feel badly if they say no."

"Why would they say no?"

"I'm not sure. Maybe because I'm not a member of this church."

"Hello?" a man in jeans and a sweater stepped out of an office. "I'm Pastor Griggs." He smiled. "I don't believe I've met you two before. Can I help you find anything?"

Vera smiled stiffly, then introduced herself and Fiona and explained their mission to recruit quilters. "I don't attend church here since I'm pretty new to Fairview. But Fiona here, she and her family come here. And perhaps I will too . . . someday. I live nearby."

"Well, considere yourself invited." He shook her hand. "We don't currently have a quilting circle here, but there used to be one back before I came on. I wouldn't be surprised if some of our members are interested in something like this." He took the poster. "What a pretty quilt. I'm happy to put this up on our bulletin board for you."

She thanked him and said she'd consider coming to his church . . . although she sensed her own insincerity. As she and Fiona hurried home, Vera felt both surprised and relieved. Hanging Nolan's posters had been much easier than she'd anticipated, and with two recruits already, it seemed to have been quite worthwhile as well. Whether or not Tasha and Eleanor were seriously interested in helping remained to be seen, but Vera found herself really hoping they were. Perhaps this quilting group was just what she needed to get out of her recent slump.

CHAPTER SIX

As Vera did some cleaning and straightening around the Albright home, she longed to remove the strange hodgepodge of furnishings and start completely over. But she knew that would be expensive and time consuming. Plus, she didn't want to overstep her bounds. Poor Kerry Albright had enough challenges on her hands with her children and surgery recovery and a husband working far from home. She didn't need to come home to find another woman had taken over and changed everything in her absence. Vera knew from experience in the design business that women—even the ones asking for help—could become very territorial and protective of their spaces. Best to tread carefully.

But Vera didn't think Kerry would object to some general tidying. And although the kitchen wasn't dirty, it could use a good scrubbing, which gave Vera something to do while Fiona took a nap. Like the rest of the house, the contents of the cupboards were sparse. They were not only short on kitchen things but food as well. This family was definitely struggling. Besides helping with the children, Vera wondered what she could do. She didn't want to offend them.

Vera had just gotten an afternoon snack laid out in her own condo when Nolan and Maureen came home from school. Shortly after they sat down, her cell phone rang. The voice of the woman on the other end was warm and cheery as she told Vera she had seen the quilt poster at her church. "My name is Beverly Clark and I've always wanted to learn to quilt. My grandmother used to run the quilters circle at our church, but she passed away ten years ago and the quilters circle seemed to go with her. Unfortunately I never had a chance to learn from her. I regret that."

Vera explained a bit more about her reason for urgency and that she already had two other women interested. "It's all happened so quickly. I'm rather taken aback."

"How many women did you plan to include in this?" Beverly asked. "Because I have several church friends who've expressed interest."

"Unfortunately my condo unit isn't very large." Vera regretted again not having her old Craftsman house—even if it was on the other side of the mountains. "So I thought four women, counting myself, would be plenty. Sometimes too many hands just complicate things."

"Yes, I suppose that makes sense. Perhaps if I learn enough from you, I'll be able to start up a quilters circle in my church someday."

"Yes, that sounds like a good idea."

They discussed the group a bit more and at Beverly's insistence, Vera agreed to plan a first-time meeting on Friday morning. "Eleven is the earliest we can meet." She explained about Tasha from the flower shop. "But I'll put together a little luncheon."

"And I'll bring an apple pie," Beverly said. "I baked several this morning."

They said their goodbyes and Vera ended the call. Meeting with her quilting group this week seemed a bit hasty, but Vera knew Kerry Albright would be home from the hospital by then. And, really, in order to finish the quilt before Christmas, Friday was not a moment too soon.

* * *

Vera found herself quite busy the next morning. After getting Nolan and Maureen off to school with neatly packed lunches, she cleaned the Albrights' master bedroom and bath and placed the worn but freshly laundered sheets back on their slightly lumpy bed. Then she got Fiona's hair neatly braided and packed a bag of street clothes for Kerry Albright to wear home from the hospital. They were just heading out the door when Tasha showed up with a colorful bouquet.

"What's this?" Vera stared at the pretty arrangement.

"I thought it might cheer up Fiona's mother." Tasha's bangle bracelets jangled as she handed the bright blooms to Vera. "Didn't you say she was coming home from the hospital today?"

"Yes. We're just going over to pick her up."

"Mama loves flowers!" Fiona's eyes grew wide. "Those are so beautiful!"

Vera handed the generously filled vase to Fiona. "Why don't you go put this on your mother's bedside table? She'll need to rest in her bedroom for most of the day. Might be nice to have something pretty to look at."

Fiona eagerly took the bouquet. As she carefully transported it back into the condo, Vera thanked Tasha for her thoughtfulness, offering to pay for it.

"No way. It's a gift." Tasha's dark eyes twinkled. "I like to salvage flowers that my aunt throws out—and she doesn't care. You know, the blooms that got beat up in transport. They might have broken stems or don't look as fresh as they should. I always try to rescue them. Either for myself or for a friend. I think they deserve a second chance, and if you arrange them just right, they're not half bad."

"Half bad? I think they looked gorgeous," Vera said. "You're a talented florist, Tasha."

"It's because I love colors and design," Tasha told her. "That's why I'm so excited about our quilting club."

"Quilting club," Vera repeated. "I like that."

"We're still on for tomorrow at eleven, right?"

"Yes. I'll provide a light lunch, and someone else is bringing apple pie."

"Sounds like a party!" Tasha wrapped her colorful scarf more snugly around her neck. "It's cold out there today. Better keep bundled up."

"That reminds me. I should get something for Mrs. Albright." She told Tasha goodbye and went back inside to find a throw blanket.

By the time Vera and Fiona got to the hospital it was nearly noon. But it still took almost an hour for Kerry to get dressed and be released. As Vera watched her being wheeled down into the foyer, she was surprised at how much prettier Kerry looked today. A bit pale and worn out perhaps, but obviously no longer in pain. Kerry smiled brightly as Fiona ran over to hug her. She let Fiona slide beside her in the wheelchair, snuggling the little girl close, but then she frowned up at Vera with a confused expression.

"I wouldn't be surprised if you don't recognize me," Vera told Kerry as she walked alongside them. "Our meeting on Tuesday was a bit stressful. But I'm your neighbor Vera Swanson. I've been caring for your children."

"Aye, I knew 'twas who you must be, but somehow you looked different to me today. Younger, I think."

Vera laughed at the memory of how haggard she'd felt the other day. "Well, that's nice to hear. And I'm sorry I didn't come to visit you yesterday, but it got too busy."

"Oh, I didn't expect you to come. I was so knackered, I dozed off most of the day." She peered up at Vera with a curious expression. "I truly thought you were very old, like my husband's mother. But you don't seem so very old to me now."

"Well, thank you very much." Vera grinned as she opened the back door, waiting as a hospital worker helped Kerry get settled in the back seat with Fiona snuggled next to her. "To be honest, I didn't recall you being this pretty the other morning. But you were in such pain."

"Such pain." Kerry sighed. "It was brutal."

"Oh, Mama." Fiona hugged her. "I'm so glad you didn't die."

Kerry tugged a pigtail. "Die? How could I die and leave my babies behind? Your mama is tougher than that, Fiona."

As Vera drove them home, she listened to Kerry and Fiona

visiting. The lilting sound of Kerry's accent was fun to hear, but hopefully she wouldn't wear herself out with her vivacious daughter. Vera would have to remind Fiona that her mother still needed quiet and rest to heal.

By the time they got into the Albright condo, Vera could see that Kerry was already getting tired. "I've got a light lunch prepared for you," she said as she walked Kerry toward the master bedroom. "I did some research on recovering from an appendectomy. You're best off with soft mild foods that don't aggravate your stomach—at least for a few days. And you're supposed to get lots of rest and no heavy lifting."

"I don't want to be treated like an invalid," Kerry argued.

"If you want to get well quicker, you'll take it easy." She pointed her toward the bed. "You get yourself comfortable while I get your lunch tray."

Vera could hear Kerry still protesting but ignored her and turned to Fiona who had followed her into the kitchen. "You stay in there with your mother. Make sure she gets into bed. She needs to rest—whether or not she thinks so. Because we want her to get better. Right?"

Fiona nodded respectfully. "Yes, so she'll get better."

Before long, Kerry was comfortably situated in her bed and no longer putting up much fuss. "Everything looks so lovely, Vera. Thank you for all you've done for me."

"You're very welcome, dear." Vera held out a tray with creamy potato soup and a small dish of applesauce on it. "Here's your lunch."

"Thanks. The flowers are so fresh and cheerful." Kerry looked teary-eyed. "So thoughtful."

"Those are from a new friend named Tasha Ellison. She

works at Susan's Flowers." Vera gently set the tray on Kerry's lap.

"Tasha is really nice and pretty," Fiona told her mother. "I like her a lot."

"Sounds like you've been having fun." Kerry tilted her head to one side. "I feel that I've missed out."

Vera tossed Fiona a warning glance, worried she might spill the beans about the Christmas quilt project, but Fiona just continued with her animated chatter, not even mentioning the quilt.

By the time Kerry finished her lunch and had taken a pain pill, it was obvious she was ready for a nap, so Vera picked up the tray and excused herself. "Your phone is right there." She pointed to the recently charged cell phone on the bedside table, which was actually a wobbly metal TV tray. "Fiona and I will be at my place until Nolan and Maureen come home from school. My phone number is in your contacts under my name—Vera. If you need anything, just call me. In the meantime, I hope you can just rest. And as soon as the kids have their after-school snack, I'll send them over to visit you."

"You're truly an angel of mercy," Kerry said sleepily. Then Vera and Fiona slipped out of the room, closing the door behind them.

"Are you really?" Fiona whispered.

Vera opened the front door and led Fiona into the hallway. "Really what?"

"An angel of mercy?"

Vera laughed. "I suppose everyone gets a chance to be an angel from time to time."

"I get to be an angel too," Fiona said as Vera unlocked her condo's door.

"You do?" She led Fiona inside.

"In the Christmas pageant at church. Most of the girls in my Sunday school class are gonna be angels too. We have to get our own costumes. Mama said she'd make me one." Fiona's brow creased. "Before she got sick . . ."

"I can help you," Vera said. "And just to reassure you, it won't be my first time making an angel costume." She remembered the time Bennett had reluctantly been an angel in a Christmas play . . . could that really have been more than thirty years ago? *My, how time flies when it comes to angel wings!*

CHAPTER SEVEN

Thanks to pressure from Fiona, Vera's condo was partially decorated for Christmas by Friday morning. The curious child had unearthed a couple Christmas bins while Vera scrounged for angel costume materials, which had been scarce. And, really, Vera was grateful for Fiona's enthusiastic urging. It was just the nudge she'd needed. And with the quilting club coming today, she figured a bit of Christmas cheer might be beneficial.

As a result, she hadn't had time to make quiche lorraine like she'd planned. But after the busyness of the morning—fixing the kids breakfast, serving Kerry fruit and oatmeal, getting Nolan and Maureen off to school, and getting Fiona to sit quietly with her mother—Vera still had time to make a quick grocery store run. And thanks to the well-stocked deli section, she had an attractive light luncheon to offer her quilting club. She was just setting it out on the breakfast bar when her first guest arrived.

To Vera's delight it was Tasha, and in her hands was another attractive bouquet. Not as lavish as yesterday's, but lovely all the same.

"Thank you, Tasha." She took the arrangement as the young woman peeled off her heavy faux fur coat and an attractive, felted hat.

"What a pretty home you have." Tasha looked around the room with appreciation. "Man, this place could be in a design magazine."

Vera thanked her and set the flowers near the food. "I was an interior designer for years. I guess old habits die hard."

"I used to think I'd like to be an interior designer." Tasha walked around the room, closely examining everything. "My style is so out there though . . . I could only work for clients who appreciate bright colors, modern art, and eclectic furnishings."

"I think that sounds delightful." Vera took in Tasha's paisley shirt over black leggings and the assortment of jewelry as she adjusted a slightly crooked lampshade. "I definitely lean toward more traditional, but I'm sure lots of people—especially younger ones—would appreciate your style."

"Maybe." Tasha sat down on the cream-colored sofa, spreading her arms out, completely comfortable. "But I decided to only share my decor style with friends."

"That's probably wise. The design business can be a pain. Some customers are impossible to please." Vera was interrupted by someone else at the door. "Excuse me." She hurried to open it, but not recognizing the portly, middle-aged smiling woman, realized she had to be the woman from the church. The covered dish in her hands seemed to confirm this.

"You must be Beverly." Vera opened the door wide.

"That's me." She presented the dish to Vera. "Here's pie."

"Wonderful. Come in." Vera introduced her to Tasha, and the bell rang again.

"That must be Eleanor." Vera set the pie down, then went to get the door.

"Is this the right place?" Eleanor asked in a somewhat brusque tone.

"Yes, of course." Vera smiled. "Welcome." She led Eleanor inside and did more introductions, but she noticed Eleanor's expression seemed laced with disapproval.

"This is such a lovely condo," Beverly said as Vera helped Eleanor remove her heavy wool coat. "I just love what you've done with the place, Vera."

"But isn't it too small for a quilting group?" Eleanor creased her brow. "I expected to find a large space with room to spread out fabrics and things. I don't see how this room can possibly contain a large quilt. And isn't that how you described it, Vera? *A large quilt?*"

"Let's all sit down and we can discuss the project," Vera said brightly. "But first, I think we should tell the group a bit about ourselves."

"Yes, that's a wonderful idea." Beverly pointed to Tasha. "I think I already know you though. You're that clever girl who works in the flower shop across from the church."

Tasha nodded. "Well, I don't know how clever I am, but yeah, I work at Susan's Flowers. Susan is my aunt."

"Susan Ellison?" Eleanor looked doubtful. "She is your aunt?"

"That's right." Tasha laughed. "Yes, I know my aunt is a freckle-faced redhead and I'm not. For the record my mom is a blond. If you're wondering where I got this dark mane of hair, you can blame it on my Jamaican father. My mom met him when she was just twenty. And, well, the result was me. Not that my father stuck around for the second act."

"Oh?" Eleanor blinked. "I see."

"How interesting." Beverly leaned forward. "Is your father involved in your life at all?"

"Nope. He doesn't even know I exist. But that's okay."

Vera nodded to Tasha. "Well, since you already got started on this, why don't you tell us a bit about yourself and why you're interested in quilting?"

"Okay. Well, I majored in art ed in college but didn't finish my degree. And I've dabbled in a lot of mediums, but I've never quilted. I do know how to sew by hand. And I'm sure if I get a real handle on quilting, I'll probably attack it from a more creative angle. Maybe free-form. But that's just me. Anyway, I had spare time and wanted something to occupy me through the winter. You know, keep me out of trouble." She laughed. "And quilting just sounds like fun. Like a bunch of pioneer women sitting around the fire and sewing."

"What a homespun image," Eleanor said, her tone brimming with sarcasm.

"Are you married, or do you have children or anything like that?" Beverly asked. "And if you don't mind me asking, how old are you?"

"I'm thirty-five." Tasha wrinkled her nose. "And thank the Good Lord, I am currently single. I was married for six years. Six lousy, miserable, wasted years. Fortunately, that's all behind me now. And no to kids, *thankfully*. Not that I don't love kids—but I was married to an overgrown kid. Anyway, for the time being, I'm living with my mom and aunt. They're both divorced too. Just one more reason I'm looking for a way to escape. Trust me, a houseful of loud-mouthed, bitter women is no picnic."

Vera and Beverly chuckled, but Eleanor remained rather grim.

"Well, I'll go next," Beverly said. "Since I asked Tasha her age, I guess I should admit I'm fifty-eight." She sighed. "Hard to believe sixty is right around the corner. I've been married to my husband, Tom, for almost forty years. Yes, we got married right out of high school. Tom's dad started Clark's Car Dealership more than fifty years ago. Tom runs it now. We have three grown sons who are living all over the world, it seems. TJ and his wife are missionaries in Mexico. They have two kids. My second son, Justin, is in the air force, stationed in Germany right now. And my baby, Adam, is out there—God only knows where—still trying to find himself." She paused with a sad expression. "But they're all good boys. So mostly I've been a mom and housewife. Well, sometimes I've done office work at the car lot. Oh yeah, and I'm active in our church."

"What made you interested in quilting?" Tasha asked.

"Oh, yes, of course. I love to sew. My grandmother had a quilting circle at the church, and I'd always meant to go and have her teach me how to quilt, but I just never got around to it. She died and the quilt group fizzled." Beverly held up her hands. "I guess I hope to revive it somehow."

"I think that's a lovely thought," Tasha told her.

"So, Eleanor, how about telling us your story?" Vera forced

a smile, hoping that this somewhat sour woman wasn't about to rain on their happy little gathering.

"Yes. Well, I'm Eleanor Rasmussen. I earned my doctorate in behavioral therapy and spent nearly forty years in private practice. My deceased husband, Rolland, was a psychiatrist. And I have one son, Evan. He's not married and probably never will be." She paused to think. "Oh, yes, I imagine I'm the oldest in our group—sixty-seven. I retired last year and am in severe need of a hobby. I'm not sure I'll be any good at quilting, although I used to sew my own clothes. But that was a long time ago."

"Thank you, Eleanor, but you're wrong about one thing," Vera said. "You're not the oldest in the group. I have you beat by one year. I'm sixty-eight. I moved to Fairview last summer to be close to my daughter and grandkids . . . after my husband passed away. But shortly after I got settled here, my daughter's husband got transferred to California." Vera sighed. "And my son and his wife live a few hours from here and they have no kids. Let's see . . . I worked in interior design for about twenty years, and I fell in love with quilting somewhere in there." She told them about the Albright family and how she'd been helping with the kids. "It was really their idea to do this. The youngest child, Fiona, is set and determined that her mama is going to get a quilt for Christmas."

"So you only just met them?" Tasha asked. "I assumed you'd known them for ages."

"I feel like I've known them for a while. But honestly, it's just this week. The mother, Kerry, is from Ireland, and the children were born there too. They all have the loveliest accents. Well, except the dad who grew up in the States." She explained how Josh worked out of town in construction. "Anyway, I wasn't so sure at first, but now I really think a big quilt would make their Christmas a bit merrier. It's just that I can't do it alone."

"There, you said it again. A *big* quilt." Eleanor waved her hand in the direction of the room. "How is that possible in here? I don't think you have space."

"I must confess that crossed my mind too," Vera admitted, "but I thought we could set up stations. A cutting area over there. Sewing in my spare room. I can move furniture in here to make room to lay it all out and—"

"And mess up your lovely room?" Beverly frowned. "I'd offer to do this at my house, but I have three overly large dogs that sort of take over."

"We will use my house," Eleanor declared.

Vera felt like they'd been hijacked. "But we—"

"It's the only logical thing to do," Eleanor insisted. "I have a very large home, and the top floor is a bonus room that's never used for anything. We can set everything up there and just leave it. You won't have to rearrange your whole house, Vera."

"What a generous offer," Beverly said. "I think it's a marvelous idea."

"Makes sense to me," Tasha agreed.

Vera shrugged. "Well, then, it sounds like a plan." She knew she should be relieved but felt disappointed. Still, she had no intention of arguing with this formidable woman. If Eleanor had said she'd been an army sergeant instead of a counselor, Vera would never have questioned it.

Now they got down to practicalities, deciding what dates

and times worked best. Everyone seemed to have a fairly flexible schedule and agreed that mornings might be best. Vera already had something of a quilting schedule in mind.

"I'll provide all the quilting tools," she said. "I have one regular sewing machine and one long arm machine that is too large to take to Eleanor's. But I can use it here. Now, if anyone else has an available machine, I think it would help."

"I'll bring mine," Beverly said.

After the details were worked out, and they settled on ten o'clock Monday morning for their first quilting session, Vera invited them to share in the luncheon. While they ate, the four of them visited fairly congenially—except for the times Eleanor spoke up. Everything from her mouth seemed to come with a barb or a question. Even as Vera began serving coffee and apple pie à la mode, Eleanor threw her wet blanket on it.

"No dessert for me, thank you." Eleanor looked down her nose at the golden pie.

"Not even just a little tiny slice?" Beverly said in a clear attempt at tempting her. "I used Gravenstein apples from my own tree. Put the filling up last summer, but the pie was fresh baked yesterday."

Eleanor held up her hands like a blockade. "One serving of that would send my cholesterol sky-high."

"Oh, well, more for us," Beverly said.

"Coffee, then?" Vera offered her a mug, hoping to reroute the conversation.

"Not for me. Caffeine would just keep me awake all night long. *No thank you!*"

"You don't worry about your cholesterol?" Eleanor challenged Beverly as they took their pie and coffee back to the sitting area.

"Well, I may be a bit on the *fluffy* side"—Beverly winked at Vera and Tasha as she sat on the sofa—"but fortunately, my cholesterol stays nice and low."

"Lucky you," Eleanor said sharply.

They had just finished dessert when Vera heard a little knock on her door. Suspecting it was Fiona since she never used the doorbell, she went to answer it. Sure enough, she was right. The little girl's braids looked a bit frazzled, and she had on a flowery dress that needed a good ironing and a black pair of slightly worn Mary Jane shoes.

"Are the quilt ladies here?" Fiona asked with a shy glance beyond Vera.

"Yes. Would you like to come in and say hello?"

Fiona nodded. "Mama's sleeping."

Vera led Fiona in, watching for the women's amused reactions. "Some of you might remember Fiona. The Christmas quilt is her idea." Vera reintroduced the women.

"Are you going to make a North Star quilt?" Fiona asked with the polite air of an almost-five-year-old.

"You mean the *Nordic* Star quilt." Vera wrapped an arm around Fiona. "But you're right, sweetie. Nordic does mean the *north* Scandinavian countries."

"What does a Nordic Star quilt look like?" Beverly asked.

"Did you see Mrs. Swanson's North—I mean, *Nordic* Star quilt?" Fiona replied.

Vera shook her head. "No, they haven't."

Fiona looked disturbed. "We must show them the quilt, Mrs. Swanson."

Vera smiled. "Why don't you do that, Fiona? You know your way around."

So Fiona, playing host and tour guide, importantly led the three women through the house. Vera lagged behind in the hallway but felt satisfied when she heard their approval of the quilt, as well as their appreciation of her craft room. When she joined them, they were already discussing colors.

"It's going to be a Christmas quilt," Fiona was telling them, "so it has to be Christmassy like this." She held up two bright bundles of cloth—one a red candy-stripe, the other a kelly-green polka-dot.

"Well, *that* will be *interesting*." Eleanor's face puckered up like she'd bitten into a lemon. "Although I'm not sure my poor eyes can handle such contrasting vivid shades."

"That's definitely very Christmassy," Vera told Fiona, "but I wonder if those are the colors your mother would really like to have in her bedroom. Remember, this quilt will be on her bed year-round, not just at Christmastime. We want her to like the colors, don't we?"

Fiona looked uncertain.

Vera reached into her bundle basket and pulled out a rich plum-colored print as well as a sage green. "Now these pieces are in the red and green family, but not quite so bright. What do you think of this?"

"Those are beautiful together." Tasha picked up a burgundy fabric and another one in mossy green, holding them like a fabric bouquet with the ones Vera had chosen. "Maybe we can work in some other shades of red and green too."

Vera added a creamy white piece to the bouquet of fabric bundles. "Perhaps something like this to set off the others."

"Ooh, that's very nice," Beverly cooed.

"I can almost imagine it," Tasha said. "It reminds me of a sweet garden in springtime. And yet it's Christmassy too." She turned to Fiona with the fabric pieces. "Do you think your mother would like these colors?"

Fiona's eyes grew wide as she nodded. "Mama likes gardens."

"What do you think?" Vera asked Eleanor.

"I'll admit it's better than that ghastly bright red and green." Eleanor grimly shook her head. "But I don't think those colors go together very well."

"Oh, I think they're wonderful," Beverly gushed. "I'd love to have a quilt with those exact same colors."

"It's a sophisticated palette," Tasha told Eleanor. "Perhaps it's an acquired taste."

"And these aren't the actual fabrics we'll use," Vera told her. "I'll have to shop for quilt fabric this weekend. This palette will simply be my guideline, but who knows what I'll find?"

"Well, I'm still not convinced. But since the majority seem to agree, I'll go along with it too." Adjusting her glasses, Eleanor scowled at the fabric pieces.

Vera and Tasha exchanged glances but said nothing. Clearly Eleanor's negativity was going to be a challenge for their little group. But now they were committed to using her house, which was probably a prudent idea, so Vera knew they'd have to make the best of it. Really, how bad could it be?

CHAPTER EIGHT

Relieved that Josh Albright had come home Friday night and planned to devote the weekend to his family, Vera felt free to spend Saturday as she pleased without concern for her neighbors. And since Tasha had expressed interest in joining her in the search for the right fabrics and quilting materials, Vera waited until afternoon since Tasha didn't get off work until two.

"I'm not sure where all the fabric stores are in Fairview," she told Tasha as they drove toward the city center. "I thought we could go to Gloria's Fabrics first."

"We could, but I wouldn't recommend it."

"Really?" Vera glanced at her. "Do you have suggestions?"

As it turned out, Tasha knew where all the craft and fabric stores were located and which ones were the best. "This is sort of like a treasure hunt," Vera told her as they perused the fourth store for just the right sage green print fabric. "Plus, it's a good way for me to see what Fairview has to offer."

After they found everything on the list, Vera offered to

take Tasha out for an early dinner. "Although," she said, "I don't really know any good places to eat."

"I know lots of great places," Tasha told her. "Depending on what you like—I like Thai and Greek and sushi restaurants."

"What's your favorite?" Vera wasn't sure how adventuresome her palate felt today.

"Well, if it were summer, I'd go for sushi or Thai. But it's such a frosty cold day, I want something warm and cozy. Comfort food, you know?"

"Sounds good to me."

"Do you like Italian?"

"I can never say no to pasta," Vera confessed.

"Martolli's has the best pesto pasta in the world. Well, Italy might have a better one, but I've never been there."

"I love pesto pasta," Vera told her.

"I knew you were a kindred spirit when I first met you." Tasha directed her to Martolli's. And because it was early in the dinner hour, they were immediately seated.

"This is so fun," Vera told her after they placed their orders. "I haven't been out to eat in months. Not since Ginny and her family moved to California."

"That must've been a blow." Tasha sipped her hot tea. "To relocate here and then have the reason for relocation go poof and disappear."

"Yes, it was sort of a shock. I never would've given up my house had I known. And to be fair, Ginny still feels badly about it. She keeps urging me to relocate to California, but I just don't see myself there. Besides the fact that real estate prices are outrageous."

"Well, despite my complaints about the climate, I actually do like Fairview." Tasha wrapped her hands around her teacup. "I guess I just wish I could travel to warm places in wintertime. Not the whole winter, because I do like the snow. But a warm break would be nice." She sighed. "Guess I'll have to marry a rich man."

"Oh, you wouldn't marry someone just for their money, would you?" Vera took a drink of her water.

"Probably not. Although sometimes when I see Mom and Aunt Susan struggling with finances, I'm not so sure. I thought I married for the right reasons the first time and look how that turned out."

"So you really married for love?"

Tasha's brow creased. "You know, I don't think anyone's ever asked me that before."

"Not even your mother?"

"Nah, she doesn't even believe in love."

"Really?" The thought made Vera sad.

Tasha nodded. "I *thought* I loved Zeke. I mean, I was pretty much smitten by him. And there's no denying he was super good-looking. Man, Zeke could charm the stripes off of a snake—like my grandma, God bless her soul, used to say. But it turns out Zeke was a snake."

"Sorry." Vera tilted her head to the side. "But that doesn't mean there's not a good guy out there. Not necessarily a millionaire, either, but someone you could love . . . someone who could love you."

"Did you have that?"

Vera nodded. "Yes, I did. Larry was one in a million. Oh, he wasn't perfect—no one is—but he was a good man. He loved me and he loved his children. And not in word only. He showed us how much he loved us all the time."

"And you really miss him, don't you?"

"More than I can even say."

"Will you ever marry again?"

Vera waved a dismissive hand. "No, I honestly don't think so."

"But what you said about love, that I could find someone to love who would love me, that doesn't apply to you?"

"You're young, Tasha. Young and beautiful and full of life. The right guy is going to find you and—"

"You don't seem old to me, Vera. The way you've been helping with your neighbors' kids and organizing the quilting club and even shopping today—honestly, you seem years younger than my mom. And she's fifty-five."

Vera smiled. "Thank you. Maybe age really is just a number. But to be honest, taking care of the Albright children this week made me feel younger and more alive, but it was also tiring. I know I'm no spring chicken."

Tasha laughed. "That's what my aunt Susan says all the time, usually when I'm trying to get her to do something fun. She's younger than my mom, but she's always saying she can't keep up with me."

"I have a feeling not many can keep up with you." Vera smiled. "You have a delightful energy, Tasha. And I'm so glad you want to be part of our quilting club. We old ladies need your youth and enthusiasm. And I don't know if you noticed or not, but little Fiona adores you. When you suggested the quilt color scheme, I expected her to balk, but you had her practically eating out of your hand. Thank you for doing that."

Tasha sighed. "She's such a sweetie pie. I hope she'll come to our quilting sessions sometimes."

"I plan to bring her Monday. That way her mother can keep resting and getting better." Vera shook her head. "That little family just breaks my heart."

"How so?"

"They're struggling so hard to get by. Kerry, that's the mom, told me they're strapped to just pay the rent, but it was the only place they could find in town. Their cupboards are pretty bare, and their furniture—well, if you can call it that—consists of plastic lawn chairs and TV trays. It's all so sad. I'd really like to help them but I'm not sure how."

Tasha's brow creased. "Yes, that can be tricky. Some people see help as charity. I remember when this one neighbor lady tried to help Mom and me. It, uh, wasn't pretty."

"Yes, I've wondered about that too."

"But if you talked to Kerry, maybe she'd be open to help. After all, you're already helping with her kids. She doesn't seem to mind that."

"That's true. And her husband, Josh, was appreciative too. He seemed genuinely grateful when he came in last night."

Tasha took another sip of tea, and it looked like she was trying to work out her next words carefully. Finally, she broke the silence. "There is one thing I noticed. I hate to even mention it, but it concerns me."

"What's that?" Vera noted Tasha's creased brow.

"Well, Fiona never seems very warmly dressed. That thin

little pink jacket she was wearing the other day doesn't seem appropriate for our cold weather."

Vera nodded. "I've had the exact same thoughts. And not only for Fiona. Nolan and Maureen both have lightweight windbreakers too. I think it's because they came up here from Arizona. The move was rather sudden. They probably had a lot of expenses. And then Kerry got sick."

"I wish I could help without hurting anyone's feelings."

"Maybe we can think of a way to keep it from feeling like charity." Vera understood what Tasha meant by offending them. That was the last thing she wanted to do. "I wonder if we could do it anonymously."

"It's something to think about. Maybe little Fiona can help us." Tasha's brown eyes twinkled. "I get such a kick out of that child. It'll be fun having her in our quilting group on Monday."

"I hope so. I dug out a quilt coloring book to help occupy her. And I might even put together some kind of sewing project for her to work on. I don't want her to get bored."

"Any plans for keeping Eleanor, aka Mrs. Scrooge, from marching us all in her gloom and doom Christmas parade?"

Vera couldn't help but laugh. "I honestly don't know what to make of that woman."

"Talk about a glass half empty person."

"Especially for a therapist." Vera shrugged. "I have a feeling she's been through something hard."

"Maybe so, but I feel sorry for all the people she counseled. They probably had to get therapy to recover from her."

Vera shook her head. "I get the impression Eleanor could use a good counselor herself."

"Maybe our quilting club will be a good influence on her. Hope springs eternal."

"See, that's what I like about you, Tasha. You're definitely a glass half full person. I need that kind of optimism in my life right now."

The two of them visited congenially throughout a delicious dinner. Vera hadn't enjoyed herself this much since first moving to Fairview. And by the time she drove Tasha home to the little house behind the florist shop, which she shared with her aunt and mother, Vera felt they were building a strong foundation for a good friendship—and it gave her hope. Oh, it wasn't that Tasha could replace Ginny. But it did help to have a young person—so full of life—around. And unless she was mistaken, Vera felt Tasha might appreciate some maternal nurturing . . . and Vera still had plenty to give.

CHAPTER NINE

Tasha wasn't surprised to take flak from her mom for joining an "old ladies quilting circle," as she put it, but she felt blindsided by Aunt Susan's negativity. "I really don't see the attraction of making a quilt with a bunch of strangers." Aunt Susan rehung the work schedule she'd just rearranged in order to accommodate the quilting sessions. "It just doesn't seem like you to me. You're more hip than that."

"I just want to learn to quilt," Tasha said, "and this is cheaper than taking a class—as in, it's free. The woman leading the group is really sweet and I can tell she's lonely. Plus, she's a very experienced quilter. Does that answer your question?"

"I guess." Aunt Susan shrugged. "At least you can still open for us in the morning."

"Wouldn't want to deprive you and Mom of your beauty sleep," Tasha teased.

"Well, it's not like this is our busy season anyway. And if

the quilting thing falls flat, you can always go back to your old hours, right?"

"Sure." Tasha pulled on her parka. "But I might discover that making quilts is fabulous and just the medium I've been searching for. I've already been imagining some designs I'd like to try—after I've learned some quilting tricks. If they're any good, maybe we could hang them in here to sell." She pointed to the empty white wall beside the floral cooler. "Might add some color to the place—especially in winter."

Her aunt seemed to consider this. "Sure, why not." She patted Tasha's head with a patronizing grin on her face. "You have fun with your little old ladies, honey. Don't do anything I wouldn't do." She laughed.

Tasha didn't appreciate the tone and could've easily tossed back a snarky reply, but she kept her thoughts to herself. At least Aunt Susan had agreed to the schedule change. And it was possible that she was right. Tasha might regret being part of this group. Especially if cranky old Eleanor Rasmussen continued to rag on everyone and everything. Of course, Tasha realized Eleanor's bad behavior might make her dig in her heels even deeper because, for some reason, she felt protective of Vera. She would probably remain in the group if only to stand by her.

As Tasha went outside, she considered riding her bike over to Eleanor's house, but according to her phone's GPS, the house was less than a mile away. And since it was a clear and sunny day, albeit cold, a brisk stroll sounded good. As she walked toward Eleanor's neighborhood, she noticed how the houses gradually grew bigger and fancier and probably a lot more expensive. Not that it was surprising. Eleanor had seemed like the sort of lady who'd live in a snooty neighborhood. Hopefully she wouldn't treat the quilting club gals like inferior peasants.

She reached Eleanor's tall brick house sooner than expected, but, chilled to the bone, Tasha had no intention of standing out in the cold to wait until ten o'clock. As she walked down the paved path, the yard looked formal and unfriendly with its perfectly sculpted hedges and short-cut lawn. No flowerpots or window boxes graced the residence, but then again, it was winter. Even so, Tasha doubted anything cheerful bloomed here *ever*. Eleanor probably disliked "messy" flowers. Tasha stared up at the tall oak door. Rather than welcoming her, it seemed to say "go away." Everything about this place seemed to reflect its owner. Hard, cold, austere. All it needed was a pair of snarling gargoyles flanking the front steps. Just the same, Tasha pressed the doorbell, imagining a sinister-sounding gong inside, and braced herself for what came next.

"Hello?" A lanky guy with shaggy brown hair stuck his head out the door. He removed his glasses then rubbed the bridge of his nose and stared at her with a puzzled expression. "You selling something, or something?"

"Uh, is this the Rasmussen house?" She rechecked the address she'd put into her phone.

"Yeah. Who're you looking for?"

"Eleanor Rasmussen," she stated a bit sharply. "I'm here for the, uh, quilting club."

His brows arched with interest. "Really?" Suddenly he stepped back and opened the door wider. "Eleanor's my mom. She's upstairs right now. In the bonus room." He chuckled. "Not sure why they call it that. Maybe the bonus was that no one has ever used it for anything. Anyway, I guess that's where you quilter ladies are going to do your sewing."

"Right." As she tugged off her leopard faux fur–trimmed gloves, Tasha could feel him giving her a once-over. Probably, just like her aunt, he didn't think she was quilting circle material. Well, whatever! "So, should I go up there now? I mean, to the bonus room." She glanced around the formal but rather stark foyer and suddenly felt out of place in her puffy purple down coat, lace-up boots, and holey jeans. Feeling nervous about her appearance was uncharacteristic for her, but this place made her feel like she should be wearing heels and hose. Not that she ever did that.

"I guess that's up to you." He leaned against the stair railing, partially blocking the steps. "Beard the lion in her den." His eyes twinkled with mischief.

Determined not to be intimidated, she stood up straighter. "It's just that I realize I'm a little early. I walked over and got here quicker than expected. It's only 9:50 right now. I don't want to disturb your mother if she's busy."

His half smile seemed to suggest he understood her hesitation. "Well, you can wait down here until ten o'clock sharp if you like."

She glanced around, wondering where he meant for her to wait. There was a pew-like bench in the foyer. Did he expect her to sit there like a child waiting to be summoned into the principal's office? She slowly unzipped her parka. "Your mother won't mind?"

He shrugged. "Who knows?" He strolled over to a pair of tall wooden doors, sliding one open.

"So, do you live here with her?" She peeled off her coat and draped it over one arm.

"Yup. Down in the basement." He waved her into a room lined with floor-to-ceiling bookcases filled with an assortment of novels.

"Oh." She went in. "That's a lot of books."

"My parents were both academics . . . books were a big deal."

"Right. I heard your dad was a psychiatrist."

"This library was Dad's favorite room. Kinda overwhelming at first, but I like it in here." He waved his hand for her to sit down. "A lot of people think it's funny that Dad was a shrink and Mom was a therapist . . . like I should've turned out better." He let out a weak-sounding laugh. Like it wasn't really a joke.

But now Tasha's stomach twisted. What was he suggesting? Like he was some sort of nutcase that his mom kept locked in the basement. "You, uh, you seem like you turned out okay." She tried to keep the question out of her tone. "Of course, I've only just met you." She smiled nervously as she eased herself into one of the oversized leather chairs.

"Thanks, I think." He chuckled as he sank easily into the other.

As he slung a long leg over his chair's arm, Tasha perched on the edge of her seat, like she was ready to bolt. She wasn't usually this uneasy, but something about Eleanor's house and this basement-dwelling son . . . well, it was a bit unnerving.

"My name's Tasha," she said politely. "Tasha Ellison."

"Tasha. That's a pretty name. Sorry, I should've introduced myself earlier. I'm Evan." He looked evenly at her.

"You seem sort of young for this quilting club biz. I kind of expected older women. You know, more like my mom's age."

"Well, I'm the youngest of our little group. But I think I'd like to try quilting as an art form, you know, like fabric sculpture or cloth collage. More free-form and expressive."

"Yeah, that was my first impression of you. That you looked like the artistic type."

"Really?" She tilted her head to one side. "What made you think that?"

"Oh, I don't know." He swung his leg off the chair's arm and sat up straight. "I suppose it was your colorful scarf and jewelry . . . or maybe it was your boots."

She glanced down at her tall laced-up boots and holey skinny jeans that were tucked into mismatched boot topper socks. "Yeah, I guess I look a little unconventional, huh?"

Evan glanced down at his own garb. Pale blue oxford shirt, neat dark pants, and brown loafers. Other than his messy hair, he looked pretty conventional. "You probably assumed I'm an accountant or something mundane like that."

"Oh, I don't know. I mean, I didn't really think about it."

"Well, if you did, you'd be right." He grinned. "I am an accountant."

"That's nice." Tasha didn't think she'd ever met an accountant before. Not exactly the crowd she hung with. But to each their own, right?

"Believe me, I don't always look this buttoned-up. It's just that I have to meet with a new client this morning. Most of the time you'll find me in a ratty rocker T-shirt and my favorite ripped jeans. My mom hates that look, but I do it anyway. Partly to get her goat." He chuckled.

"Uh-huh." She really didn't know what to make of this guy, or why he was telling her all this. Glancing at her phone she was relieved to see it was now three minutes to ten. Hopefully someone else would come early too. "So, if you, uh, have a client this morning, shouldn't you be heading for work?"

"My office is down in the basement," Evan continued. "There's a private exit so my clients can come and go without disturbing my mother. But when I heard the bell, I thought maybe my client got mixed up." He checked his watch. "Although he's not due here until ten thirty."

"Oh." She nodded, trying to think of something to say.

"Living down there gives us space. Especially now that Mom's retired. I try not to disrupt her peace and quiet." He rolled his eyes as if to suggest he'd like to do some disrupting.

"So you live *and* work in the basement?" She frowned to imagine him down in some dark, dreary dungeon. Talk about cabin fever.

"Yeah, it's not too bad. I have a studio apartment with a mini kitchen and everything I need. There's even a separate office to receive clients. But best of all, I have a soundproof rehearsal room."

"Rehearsal room?" She imagined him as a concert pianist. Eleanor would probably approve of that.

"Yeah, for my band to practice."

"You have a band?"

"Sure. We've been doing music together since high school. Well, off and on, anyway. Lately we've been more on than off."

"What sort of music?"

He seemed to study her. "Probably not your style."

"What do you think is my style?" she asked.

"I don't know." He rubbed his chin. "Hip-hop? Pop? Mixed in with a little classical. Maybe some West Coast jazz."

"You're partly right. As a matter of fact, my taste in music is very eclectic."

"Yeah, but I'm guessing you're not into bluegrass."

"You play bluegrass?"

"Yeah, that and folk and some other stuff."

"Well, you might be surprised that I happen to like bluegrass and folk as well as classic jazz. I've even been known to listen to Frank Sinatra. It all depends on my mood."

"That's cool."

"So does your band ever play around here?"

"Yeah. We do weddings and parties. More in the summer. But we have a couple of gigs lined up for the holidays. Do you ever go to—"

"Hello?"

Tasha looked over to the still-open library doors to see Eleanor peering in at them with a furrowed brow.

"Oh, hi." Tasha stood. "I arrived a little early, so Evan's been keeping me company."

"Why didn't you just send her upstairs?" Eleanor asked Evan, her tone sharp.

"Well, I—"

"It was my choice. I didn't want to disturb you." Tasha glanced at Evan, who just shrugged.

"Why would it disturb me for you to join me up in the room I've prepared for our group?" Eleanor demanded. "Maybe I could've used some help up there. Setting up the tables and chairs and things would've been easier with two people."

"I'm sorry. I didn't even think of that." Tasha was relieved to hear the doorbell ring. Eleanor went to get it, and Evan gave her a slightly sympathetic look.

"What can I say?" He held up his hands in a hopeless gesture. "My mother . . . well, she can be rather difficult. But I suspect you know that already."

Tasha refrained from wholeheartedly confirming his words. "Well, it was nice to meet you, Evan. Good luck with your new client—and with your music."

He suddenly reached for her hand, politely shaking it. "It was really nice to meet you too, Tasha Ellison. Hopefully we'll cross paths again."

She smiled stiffly but was surprised at the warm rush that went through her from just the touch of his hand. "Who knows?"

"Now I better skedaddle before the old ladies take over." His brown eyes twinkled. "Have fun."

As he slipped away, Tasha slowly shook her head. Evan seemed so drastically different from Eleanor. Were they truly related or was he perhaps a foundling dropped on the doorstep as an infant? Tasha used to entertain such stories for herself since she was nothing like her own flesh and blood mother. As she went back out to the foyer, she felt a surge of sympathy for Evan. To live under the same roof as Eleanor—even in the basement. That couldn't be easy. Despite having a mother like that, he seemed surprisingly laid-back. At least that's how he'd appeared, but Tasha knew from experience that first impressions could be wrong. And why was she still thinking about that nerdy accountant anyway?

CHAPTER TEN

As they unloaded bins and bags and sewing machines on and around a bench by the formal staircase, Vera could tell that their host wasn't comfortable with the disarray of so much clutter in her elegant foyer. But they needed to set things down in order to remove their coats like Eleanor had instructed them to do. One by one Eleanor hung their wraps in a rather barren coat closet equipped with sturdy wooden hangers. Vera vaguely wondered if Eleanor kept house herself or had help.

She hung Fiona's little pink coat on a hanger then handed it to Eleanor, but the expression on Eleanor's face, as she took the lightweight coat, suggested her displeasure at having a young child in her home. Vera had expected as much and already warned Fiona to mind her manners and not touch anything without permission.

"I brought freshly made chocolate chip cookies," Beverly said cheerfully. "I thought we girls might need some sustenance while we're working. Perhaps we could make some coffee to go with—"

"I have no coffee in my house." Eleanor scowled at the plastic-wrapped platter of cookies. "I don't indulge in coffee *or* sweets."

"Oh, that's right." Beverly glanced at Vera.

"Perhaps we could make some tea to go with the cookies?" Vera asked Eleanor. "Or even just a pitcher of water."

"Fine. I'll put the teakettle on." Eleanor nodded to the stairs. "Go ahead and take your things up to the third floor. The only thing up there is the bonus room. I've already set up some tables and folding chairs. And I took up some extension cords and additional lighting. I hope it's sufficient." She sighed wearily.

"I'm sure that must've been hard work, but it all sounds perfect." Vera picked up her sewing machine case. "Thank you so much, Eleanor."

"Well, I guess you can get settled up there while I see about some tea. But I'll warn you, all I have is herbal."

With everyone carrying something, they managed to get most of it up the three flights of stairs. But seeing how Beverly looked winded, Vera suggested she and Tasha go back down for the fabric bins.

"I'll help too," Fiona offered cheerfully.

Vera wasn't sure how much Fiona could carry, but when they got down to the foyer the little girl grabbed a plastic case of quilting notions and went bouncing back up the stairs like the Energizer bunny.

As Vera and Tasha gathered up the remaining bins, Tasha lowered her voice. "I wonder if this is going to be worth it."

"What do you mean? The stairs?"

"I mean *Eleanor*. She's so unpleasant. While you were setting up your sewing machine, Beverly told me her church has a large meeting room we could use."

Vera didn't know what to say.

"I'm not trying to be Debbie Downer, but I'm worried Eleanor is going to make this a miserable experience for everyone."

"Well, let's give her a chance," Vera whispered. "At least for today."

"Right."

They took the fabric bins upstairs where Beverly was already connecting sewing machines to extension cords. Vera surveyed the space and then started to organize the workstations. "Sewing over here," she told them. "Cutting here. And we'll need an iron and ironing board. I completely forgot about that. I wonder if Eleanor has anything."

"I'll go find out," Tasha said, a slightly reluctant expression on her face.

"I'll go with you," Fiona said cheerfully.

Tasha brightened. "Thank you, darling!"

After they left, Vera asked Beverly about the room at her church.

"Yes, I told Tasha about it in case it doesn't go too well with Eleanor." Beverly turned on a lamp. "I don't care to speak ill of anyone, but I get the impression she really doesn't want us here."

"I'm having similar concerns. But she was so insistent last week. It's confusing."

"I know. Maybe she just wants things her way," Beverly said, her voice low. "Some people are like that."

"That's true." Vera suspected Eleanor was accustomed to having her way.

"The only problem with the room at the church is that we'd have to take everything down and get it out after each quilting session." Beverly frowned. "Up here we could just leave everything in place. No hauling stuff back and forth." She used her hand to fan her flushed face. "Just lugging my machine up those stairs was a chore."

"I know what you mean." Vera waved an arm toward the oversized bonus room. "If we stay here, we have all this space."

Beverly shrugged. "I suppose we'll just have to make the best of it."

"It's probably too soon to give up," Vera said.

"I wonder if Eleanor needs a hand with tea things." Beverly grimaced. "I didn't mean to make more work for her. Maybe I'll bring a big thermos of coffee next time."

"Good thinking. In the meantime, I'll go down and lend a hand. You keep setting things up in here." As Vera went back down, she realized that the stairs had probably been hard on Beverly. And to be honest, she felt a bit winded herself. Hopefully this wasn't a big mistake. Already it seemed that Tasha and Beverly were having serious second thoughts about Eleanor. For that matter, Vera was too.

When she reached the first floor, Vera heard a loud crash. She rushed toward the sound of it, passing through a large formal dining room, then heard Eleanor's raised voice. "I'll have you know those teacups are antiques. You clumsy child! What made you think you could carry an ironing board by yourself?"

In the kitchen, Vera saw shards of pink-and-white china splattered across the tile floor, and Fiona, cowering with a fearful expression, clung to an ironing board with its legs splayed open.

Vera rushed to the girl's side. "What happened?"

"It's my fault," Tasha told them. "I was getting the iron from a high cabinet, and I let Fiona take the ironing board. I knew it was too big for her, but she wanted to—"

"And she rammed the works into the countertop where my teacups were stacked," Eleanor interrupted hotly. "I don't know why we need a small child here while we work." She shook her finger at Vera. "Couldn't you have gotten a babysitter?"

Ignoring Eleanor, Vera knelt by Fiona. Big tears streaked down the little girl's flushed cheeks. "It's okay, sweetie. I know you didn't mean to break anything. You were just trying to help." She wrapped her arms around Fiona and held her close. "It's okay. Please, don't cry."

Meanwhile Tasha located a broom and dustpan and was already sweeping up the broken china pieces. Fortunately, it looked to be only a couple cups and saucers. Still holding a protective arm around Fiona's shoulders, Vera stood to face Eleanor. "I'm very sorry that happened," she said tersely. "I will gladly reimburse you for the broken china."

"They're old pieces that *can't* be replaced," Eleanor snapped.

"I don't see why you were using such nice things in the first place," Tasha said as she stood with the filled dustpan. "Wouldn't paper cups be more practical?"

Eleanor glared at her. "I don't *use* paper cups."

"Well, just some everyday mugs, then?" Tasha dumped the shards into the garbage compactor that Eleanor had opened for her.

She opened a cabinet filled with less-formal dishes. "Here, then. Why don't you take care of it yourself?" Eleanor picked up the ironing board. "I'll take this upstairs to ensure nothing else gets smashed or broken on the way."

As she stormed off, Vera and Tasha exchanged concerned glances. Then Tasha knelt down to hug Fiona, holding her tightly. "Don't you let that horrible old witch scare you," she said quietly. "She doesn't really *eat* little children for her morning snack, but the neighbors should probably keep an eye on their helpless puppy dogs."

Despite disapproving of Tasha calling Eleanor a witch in front of Fiona, Vera couldn't help but smile. And to her relief, it brought a shaky grin to Fiona's face too.

"She doesn't truly eat puppies?" Fiona blue eyes grew large.

"No, honey, I'm just kidding." Tasha tugged on a blond pigtail.

"I'm sorry I broke Eleanor's dishes," Fiona said solemnly to Vera. "I didn't mean to."

"Of course you didn't," Vera reassured her.

"Everyone makes mistakes, little Fifi," Tasha said gently.

"*Fifi?*" Fiona's pale brows arched.

"That is what I'm going to call you. My little Fifi. Is that okay with you?"

Fiona beamed up at her. "Yes, yes! I like it!"

As Vera and Tasha took the tea things up, letting Fiona carry the iron, which she held very carefully, Vera hoped that the worst part of this morning was behind them. But with Eleanor's sour disposition, who could tell?

By the time they got upstairs, Beverly had set her platter of cookies on a small card table in a corner of the room, and Eleanor, on the other side of the room, was looking at the fabrics Vera and Tasha had collected for the quilt.

"Well, here we are," Vera said as she went over to Beverly. "We have a nice pot of hot peppermint tea. I thought we might all enjoy a cup while I explain a bit about the quilt-making process and assign tasks. How does that sound?" Not waiting for a response—or not wanting to give Eleanor a chance to object—Vera invited everyone to put the folding chairs in a circle and sit down.

"To start with, I'll give a demonstration on the cutting process." She held up a roller cutter, explaining how it worked. "We can all do some cutting, just to learn, but once we have enough pieces to begin sewing, Tasha will take full charge of cutting. Eleanor and Beverly will each work on their machines to piece the parts together. I'll take charge of ironing the seams open, which will allow me time to check the work as well as float between the stations to make sure everyone understands what we're doing. Does that make sense?"

"How will we know which pieces to sew and how to sew them?" Beverly asked.

"We'll number each piece during cutting, and then we'll pin them together. You'll sew number one piece to number two and number two to number three and so on. And for a visual, I've drawn and colored some patterns so you can see what the squares will eventually look like." She pulled out the drawings she'd sketched the night before. "But the numbers will help us to get our geometry right. It's funny, I never cared for math in school, but quilting is actually quite mathematical."

"So those are really the colors we're using?" Eleanor scowled.

Vera lifted up the yardage that she'd prewashed and ironed yesterday. "Yes, Tasha and I feel these colors look very nice together. Don't you?"

"I love them," Beverly said quickly. "I'd be thrilled to have a quilt with those colors on my bed."

"We thought it was Christmassy without being over the top."

Eleanor crossed her arms in front of her with an unconvinced expression. "I just don't think those colors go with the Nordic Star pattern. I would think Nordic colors would be preferable. More authentic."

"What are true Nordic colors?" Tasha asked her.

"Well, like red and blue and white. Like their flags."

Tasha pulled out her phone, then punched something in. "According to this website, Nordic colors aren't limited to red, white, and blue." She held up her phone to show them a palette of muted earth tones, including some that were very similar to the fabrics.

"Well, I—"

"We could put it to a vote," Beverly suggested, "but it looks like three of us are already happy with these colors."

"I like them," Fiona chimed in. "And I know Mama will like them too."

Vera grinned. "Then that settles it." She continued her quilting tutorial, taking time to answer a few more questions, then demonstrated how the rotary cutters and self-healing mats worked. Then with Beverly and Eleanor looking on, she and Tasha cut out enough shapes to get the sewers to sewing. To Vera's relief, Fiona occupied herself with coloring a quilt picture. And since her last protest about colors, Eleanor became surprisingly quiet. Vera wondered if she felt guilty for her tantrum down in the kitchen.

By the time the women started sewing, Fiona had grown bored with coloring. Vera had expected as much and brought along a "sewing basket," which included colorful yarn, an oversized needle, and some scraps of loosely woven fabrics and felt shapes in Christmas colors. She was just setting Fiona up for "sewing" when Eleanor called out to Vera.

"I just don't see how these two pieces go together. It should be number five next to number six, right? But it's not working. Tasha must've cut them wrong."

"Just a moment," Vera called back.

"Ouch." Fiona jabbed her thumb with the needle. Fortunately, it wasn't sharp enough to draw blood, but probably hurt.

"You have to watch where you poke that thing." Vera showed her how to safely place her hands. "Like this." She watched as Fiona took another stitch without pain then helped her to pull the red yarn all the way through the green felt. "Perfect," Vera proclaimed. "Now just keep going around the edges until the green circle doesn't come off the burlap."

"*Vera!*" Eleanor snapped. "Are we here to teach infants to sew or to make a silly quilt in time for Christmas?"

"I'm coming." Vera wanted to point out that Eleanor

seemed more like a child than Fiona but kept her thoughts to herself.

"See." Eleanor held up her piece. "They do not fit."

"It's because this one is upside down," Vera replied.

"No, it's not."

"Yes, it is. That's why this side is long and that's short." Vera pulled a seam ripper from her pocket and took the pieces apart. "Also, these seams should be ironed open before you attach this piece." She pointed out how the edges were in the way.

"Well, you left your station by the iron," Eleanor said, crossing her arms.

"Surely, you know how to iron open your own seams." Vera tried to keep the aggravation out of her voice.

"Of course, but I thought you were in charge of the iron."

"In time, we should all be ironing our own seams. In fact, I think I'll bring my own iron over so we can have two ironing stations. I'll just set it up with a towel on a table."

"I can bring an iron too," Beverly offered. "Lord knows I never use it at home anymore." She chuckled. "That's one thing I taught my boys to do for themselves. Before they ever left home, all three of them knew how to do their own laundry *and* ironing too. Their wives can thank me for that. At least TJ's wife can. He's the only married one and Tess tells me he does the ironing for both of them. Can you believe that?"

"Amazing." Eleanor's tone dripped with sarcasm.

Without missing a beat, Beverly continued, "Now my Tom, bless his heart, still takes his shirts to the cleaners. But then you know how car salesmen always have to look nice and neat at work. When we first got married my ironing was a great disappointment to him." She laughed. "He still doesn't know I did it on purpose just to keep him going to the dry cleaners. But don't you girls go telling on me."

Vera and Tasha laughed, but Eleanor looked irritated. It wasn't the first time Beverly had entertained them with her long-winded family tales. Vera thought it helped to lighten the mood, but she suspected Eleanor preferred silence.

Beverly, probably encouraged by their laughter, launched into another story about her boys' housekeeping skills, telling how TJ accidentally put dish soap in the washing machine as a teenager, but she had barely gotten to the overflowing suds part when Eleanor stood up with clenched fists.

"Beverly, must you talk nonstop?" she asked loudly.

"Well, I—no, of course not." Beverly pursed her lips. "I just think it helps to pass the time."

"Maybe it passes your time," Eleanor said, "but not mine."

Vera took in a slow deep breath. "You must've spent a lot of time listening to people during your counseling career, Eleanor . . . hearing them going on and on about their troubles. I'm sure it got tiresome."

"Maybe that's why she's so cranky about it now," Tasha said.

"I'm *not* cranky," Eleanor snapped. "I just enjoy a little peace and quiet. I erroneously assumed that quilting would be a quiet sort of hobby."

"I've often imagined what it was like for pioneer women, you know, when they gathered to work on quilts," Vera said in an attempt to change the subject. "Can you imagine how isolated a woman might feel out on a farm? Sure, she was caring for children and a husband, but what about having someone to chat with? And their daily chores—cooking on woodstoves, carrying water from the well, milking cows, churning butter, growing and putting up vegetables—well, it must've been exhausting . . . and lonely. Getting together with other women, sitting for a whole day just stitching a quilt top, well, it probably felt like a vacation. And such a special social occasion. They must've looked forward to it for weeks. I'll bet they brought good things to eat too, and the conversation must have flowed freely as they caught up on the latest news."

"Yes, that's how I've envisioned it too," Tasha agreed. "Kind of like a girls' night out in the daytime." She laughed. "And with no regrets the next day."

"I remember the first time I got to visit my grandma's quilting circle as a little girl," Beverly said. "I was probably about Fiona's age and so in awe of these ladies all stitching away and visiting together. I still remember sitting under the quilting frame just listening to them chatter away."

"What a fun memory," Tasha said.

"And something I'd love to reinvent." Beverly glanced at Eleanor with an uneasy expression. "Women enjoying women's company and creating something."

The room grew very quiet now and Vera got an idea. "Wouldn't it be nice to have some Christmas music up here while we work?" she suggested. "To keep our mood merry and bright."

"Yes." Tasha grabbed her phone. "I'll create a holiday playlist right now."

"Perfect. And make sure you get some old Christmas carols too," Beverly said. "Then we could sing along."

Eleanor made a grunt of disapproval but said nothing.

It didn't take long for Tasha to get Christmas tunes playing. Although the music was nicer than silence, Vera would've preferred happy conversation. Not that it seemed possible with Eleanor always throwing a wrench into the works. Vera tried to mentally calculate just how many hours they'd be forced to spend in Eleanor's company in order to complete this quilt. As she pinned a burgundy square to a sage square, she decided to sew more blocks at home. She wouldn't mention it to anyone, or her eagerness to expedite the process. Suddenly her hurry had nothing to do with Christmas coming.

CHAPTER ELEVEN

As much as Tasha disliked being in Eleanor's company, she was determined to see the quilt project through to its completion. For Vera's sake as well as Fiona and her mother's. Still, she found herself gritting her teeth as she rang Eleanor's doorbell on Wednesday morning—bracing herself for their second quilting session.

"Hello." Evan opened the door wide. "I thought it might be you."

"Really?" She went inside.

"Yeah, the other ladies are already here." He grinned. "You're late."

She held up her to-go cup. "Because I stopped for a mocha."

"Yum." He stuck out a hand. "How about I hold that while you take off your coat?"

"Can I trust you?" she teased.

"I'm not sure, but I'll try to control myself." He took the cup and sniffed it. "Have you tried peppermint mocha?"

"No, but it sounds good."

He smacked his lips. "Yeah, now I'm craving one."

As she peeled off her coat, Tasha observed that Evan didn't look so buttoned-up today. Like her, he wore ragged jeans. And his gray sweatshirt looked ancient. Even his moccasin slip-ons were well worn. He looked casually comfortable. At home in his own skin.

"So, what are you doing up here?" She traded her coat for her coffee, then waited while he hung it up for her. "Thought you'd be down in your dungeon."

"Dungeon?" He tilted his head to one side. "Is that what you think?"

She shrugged then sipped her coffee.

"Maybe I should give you a little tour of my digs."

She glanced upstairs then shrugged again. "Why not? I'm already late."

"Come on, then." He tugged her arm, taking her around a corner and down a hallway. With a mysterious chuckle, he opened a door. "Let me take you to my dungeon," he said in a Dracula-like voice. As he led her down a steep, narrow stairway, he continued the act. "Vatch your step, my little pretty. My treacherous stairs are meant to discourage unvanted guests."

She laughed, but not wanting to careen headfirst into him, took it easy down the dimly lit stairs. Once they got all the way down, she noticed sunlight streaming through some high windows. She stepped into a well-laid-out kitchen and living space. "This is really nice." She ran her hand over the gleaming granite countertop. "Not very dungeon-like."

"Or Dracula's lair?"

"Too light and bright." She took in the small stainless steel fridge, microwave, and dishwasher. "And all the comforts of home."

"My mom really wanted me back home after my dad died so she pulled out all the stops on this place. I moved back last summer." He opened the door to an office with an exterior glass door. "This is where I work."

"Nice." She nodded approvingly.

He opened another door, exposing a spacious bathroom that looked surprisingly neat for a bachelor and then a door to a bedroom where the bed was actually made. "I'm impressed with your housekeeping skills," she admitted as he led her to another door.

"Thanks. But to be honest, my mom has a housekeeper who comes down here once a week, so I can't take all the credit."

"Pretty posh." She wanted to say spoiled but suspected that judgment had more to do with Eleanor than Evan. She suddenly remembered something Eleanor had said at their first meeting, that she never expected Evan to marry. Maybe she just wanted to keep him at home.

Evan opened the door to a large room with heavily insulated walls and a variety of musical instruments scattered about.

"Your practice room?"

"Yep." He looked satisfied. "Not bad, eh?"

"Not bad at all." She considered the crowded bedroom she shared with her mother in Aunt Susan's cramped house. It would fit into one corner of this practice room. "But I'm curious. You said your mom wanted you to come back home to live. Back home from where?"

"Oh, just an apartment downtown. Nothing much. But my own space. Ya know?"

"Yeah." She nodded like she knew, but the truth was she'd never had her own space. Not really. But at least her aunt had allowed her to use the attic for a studio. A seasonal studio since half the time it was an oven or a deep freezer.

"Well, I probably shouldn't keep you from your quilting ladies," he said with what sounded like reluctance.

"Yeah, they'll probably give me hecky-pecky." She chuckled.

As he walked her back up the stairs, he started talking about good coffee places in town, asking her which was her favorite.

"The truth is, I've only been in Fairview a year. I've been getting coffee at the place near my aunt's flower shop, where I work."

"My favorite spot is City Brew. It's downtown, near where my office used to be. That's where I discovered peppermint mocha." He leaned against the stair banister. "And I, uh, I wondered if maybe I could take you there, uh, sometime."

She paused on the first step, turning to look at him. "Are you asking me out, Evan Rasmussen?"

He nodded with a sheepish expression. "Yeah, I guess I am."

"Well . . ." She studied him, then nodded her approval. "Then my answer is I think I'd like that."

He beamed at her. "I have a client coming this afternoon. But I'm free after four. Does that work? Or is it too soon?"

"That sounds great." She pulled out her phone and they exchanged numbers. As she pocketed her phone, Evan promised to pick her up at the flower shop shortly after four. She thanked him for the tour of his basement abode, and as she hurried upstairs, her feet felt light and her heart felt hopeful. Evan was nothing like the kind of guys she usually dated—or the one she accidentally married. In fact, Evan was slightly nerdish. Not the sort of bad boy type that normally turned her head. And yet he had.

* * *

Although Vera was glad to see Tasha show up, she hated to hear Eleanor tear into her. "I always told my clients it's selfish to be late and that their time wasn't theirs alone," she lectured. "And, of course, I always charged them for the full hour anyway."

"Of course," Tasha muttered as she picked up the roller cutter. "I guess you could always charge me too, Eleanor. Except, oh yeah, I'm doing this for free."

"Good point, Tasha." Beverly chuckled. "There's banana nut bread on the snack table over there. Baked it last night."

"And it's really good," Vera said.

"Sounds great." Tasha continued cutting. "As soon as I stockpile enough pieces here, I'll try it."

"How about that Christmas music?" Vera asked after a short stint of silence.

"Yes. I nearly forgot. I added a lot of artists last night." Tasha held up her phone. "Everything from Bing Crosby to Ariana Grande to Eminem."

"M&Ms?" Eleanor frowned. "Singing candy?"

Tasha and Beverly both laughed—loudly.

"Eminem is a rapper," Beverly said when she'd pulled

herself together. “My boys used to listen to him. Tom hated his music. I wouldn’t think he’d do Christmas songs.”

“Rap music? Not in my house,” Eleanor said sharply.

“I’ll side with Eleanor on this,” Vera said. “I don’t care for rap.”

“I was kidding,” Tasha assured them. “I didn’t really put rap on my Christmas playlist. And I’m pretty sure you gals wouldn’t like Eminem.”

“Although M&Ms sound good,” Beverly said. “I used to make cookies with holiday M&Ms. The kids loved them. Maybe I’ll bring some for our next session.”

Eleanor let out a loud groan. “Do you not understand how bad sugar is for you, Beverly? I’m surprised you’re not diabetic by now.”

“You and my doctor both.” Beverly chuckled. “But my blood sugar levels are perfectly normal. Not so much for poor Tom. He’s still as skinny as the day we got married, but pre-diabetic.”

“Probably from all the sweets you shove at the poor man,” Eleanor snapped.

“Oh, I never leave those goodies around *my* house,” Beverly told her. “I give them to friends and neighbors, and I take them to church on coffee hour days.”

“Right. Poison your friends.” Eleanor shook a finger at Beverly. “You’re a pusher.”

Beverly’s smile dissolved, and she looked close to tears. And who could blame the poor woman? Vera was about to defend her, but Beverly spoke up in a slightly quivering voice “I’ll have you know that since my boys left home, I rarely bake anymore. But December comes around and I can't seem to help myself. I'm compelled to make cookies and nut breads and all sorts of things. But no one I give them to ever complains." She tilted her head to one side. "Well, except for you, Eleanor."

"Well, I for one have enjoyed your treats, Beverly." Vera set down the iron and went over to her, placing a hand on Beverly's shoulder. "It puts me in a jolly, Christmassy mood."

Tasha held up her phone. "And to add to our Christmassy state of mind, here's Dean Martin singing 'A Marshmallow World.'" She put the phone where everyone could hear. After that song ended, "Deck the Halls" came on, and Beverly, in her lilting voice, began to sing along. Soon Tasha and Vera were singing too. But not Eleanor. With her head bent over the sewing machine and tight-lipped exasperation visible in her expression, she continued to sew.

By quitting time, Vera was pleased with how much they'd gotten done, but it was still dismaying to consider how much remained. Despite her resolve to get more blocks done at home, she'd been so distracted with helping the Albright children the past couple of days that there'd been little time for sewing. Although Kerry claimed to be on the mend, she seemed very weak and weary and perhaps even depressed. As a result, Vera continued to help out. And it wasn't an imposition. The truth was she loved spending time with the children. Although she wanted Kerry to get well, she didn't mind that it was taking longer than expected. Otherwise she'd have no excuse to remain this involved in their lives.

* * *

Tasha was just finishing an arrangement for a new mother when the bell on the front door jingled. She looked up to see Evan coming in. He wore a leather bomber jacket and a curious expression. “So this is where you work?” He nodded his approval. “I like it.”

“Thanks.” She slid in the last of the pink rosebuds then held up the vibrant bouquet, turning to inspect all sides. “I’m almost done.”

“That’s nice.”

“It’s for Serena and Baby Olivia.” She reached for her jacket. “Since we’re going downtown for coffee, would you mind letting me drop it off at St. Luke’s Hospital on the way?”

“Not at all.” He grinned. “Good thing I didn’t bring my motorcycle.”

“You have a motorcycle?” She wound her knitted scarf around her neck.

He nodded. “But I don’t ride it when it’s icy. My mom thinks I’m crazy to ride it at all, but I’m not that crazy.”

Tasha could easily imagine the opinionated Eleanor tearing into Evan for having a motorcycle. “You and your mom aren’t much alike, are you?” She tucked the arrangement into a tissue paper–lined box then called out goodbye to her aunt in the back room.

“I guess I’m more like my dad.” Evan held the door open for her. “But to be fair, my mom wasn’t always like she is now.”

Tasha used her arm to shelter the flowers from the frosty wind that whipped against them as Evan hurried to open the door of a small electric car. “Here you go.” He waited for her to get in and then closed the door. When was the last time a guy had done that for her?

After he got inside, she turned to look at him. “What did your mom used to be like?”

He pursed his lips as he pulled out into the street. “She was just your ordinary mom type. I mean, yeah, she had her career, but she always tried to keep her family first. And she used to actually be fun.”

Tasha could not imagine Eleanor ever being fun. “Was it losing your dad that changed her?”

“That was part of it.” He sighed. “It was a hard blow, for sure. She and my dad had been planning for retirement. You know, all the things they’d been putting off. They were pretty compatible, so it was a big loss. But there’s more to it than that.”

Tasha shifted in her seat to face him. “What do you mean?”

“My sister . . . Emily.” Evan’s brow creased as he stopped at a red light.

“I didn’t realize you have a sister.”

“*Had* a sister.”

Her stomach twisted into a knot. “Oh?”

“Emily was seven years younger than me. She and my mom were like best friends.”

“That had to be hard.”

“Yep. Emily had just graduated college. She followed my parents’ example by getting her psych degree. They were pretty proud of her. I was too. Anyway, Em was out riding her bike on just a normal summer day, and in a freak accident, she was run down by a teen girl who was texting while driving. Died instantly.”

"That's horrible. I'm so sorry."

"Yeah. That was hard, for sure. A few months later, Dad got diagnosed with pancreatic cancer. He died almost exactly a year after Emily."

"Wow, what a tragic year for you and your mom."

"Yeah. She took it pretty hard. We both did."

"That must be why she needed you to move back home." Tasha felt a surprising pang of compassion for Eleanor.

"I guess I wanted to move back too." He cleared his throat loudly as he turned into the hospital entrance, then pulled up to the drop-off area. "If you're quick, I'll wait here."

"I'll be right back." As she made her way to the reception desk, Tasha felt such sadness for Evan and Eleanor. To lose two family members in a year. No wonder Eleanor was so unhappy. Tasha handed over the flowers then hurried back out to the car.

"Thank you for telling me about your family," she said quietly. "It helps me to understand your mom better."

"I don't usually tell people about all that. Not so early on in a, uh, friendship, anyway. But I thought you deserved to know. I mean, since you're in Mom's quilting group. I know her negativity can drive people nuts sometimes. I wouldn't want her scaring you away."

"Fortunately, I don't scare that easily." She smiled. "But if you don't mind, I'd like to let the other quilting gals in on this. It might make them more understanding."

"Fine by me. I'm not sure what Mom would think, but maybe it doesn't matter." He snagged a parking spot right in front of the coffee shop. "Here we are."

As they went inside, Tasha was still pondering his family's pain, but determined to make this date a happy one, she changed the subject. "What a beautiful Christmas tree." She paused to sniff the tall tree by the door. "It's real too."

"There should be a law against fake trees," he said as he unzipped his jacket.

"My aunt wants to put a fake tree in the flower shop." Tasha glumly shook her head. "I don't get it. I mean, we don't sell fake flowers."

"Want to get your aunt a real tree?" Evan's blue eyes lit up. "I know a great place. It's where my family used to go . . . back when we were still a family."

"I'd *love* to get a real tree!" She clapped her hands together.

"Are you free on Saturday?" he asked.

She assured him she'd make sure she was free, and it was settled. On Saturday morning, they would go to the tree farm together. "I'll get a tree for my house too," he said with enthusiasm. "We didn't have one last year, and it was pretty depressing."

"Is your little car big enough for two trees?"

"I'll take my dad's SUV. It just sits in the garage anyway."

As they sipped peppermint mochas together, Evan told her about Christmases in the past—how his mom decorated the whole house and friends and relatives would pour in. "I've got some great memories." His shoulders slumped. "But I don't expect to ever experience that again. Not in my house, anyway. Last Christmas was bleak."

"Maybe getting a tree will help your mom feel like celebrating," she suggested. But she could tell by his expression, he was as doubtful as she. Tasha considered herself an imaginative person, but for the life of her, she could not imagine Eleanor Rasmussen in a festive mood. Still, it would be fun to get trees with him. In fact, it'd be fun to do a lot of things with Evan.

CHAPTER TWELVE

Vera's plan for Saturday was to sew as many quilt blocks as possible, but it wasn't even nine o'clock yet when the Albright children began to trickle in. It started with Fiona bringing in Vera's newspaper. Then Maureen came by to ask about making Christmas cookies. "Didn't you say we could make them with you?"

"Yes, dear," Vera said patiently, "I said that, but I think we should wait about a week. You know, until it's closer to Christmas."

Maureen nodded, but her big brown eyes showed disappointment. Vera was about to rethink cookie-making when her doorbell rang again. It was Nolan this time.

"Maureen said you're making Christmas cookies today." He looked up hopefully. "Care for any help?"

"Well, more hands do make lighter work." As Vera turned off her iron, she tried to remember if she had all the ingredients for her traditional sugar cookies. She was just leading the children to her kitchen when the bell rang once more. "Goodness, it feels like Grand Central Station in here." She looked at Nolan. "Do you suppose that's your parents?"

"Nah," he told her. "They're sleeping in. They told us to be quiet."

"Oh, I see." Vera went to the door and was surprised to see Tasha and Eleanor's son with two large poinsettia plants in hand. "What have we here?"

"Merry early Christmas." Tasha handed her a plant. "My aunt got a surplus of these guys, and Evan and I thought maybe you could use one."

"Thank you." Vera took the gift. "It's lovely."

"I thought the Albrights might enjoy the other one in their place." She glanced past Vera. "But it seems they're over here."

"The children wanted to make Christmas cookies." Vera lowered her voice. "Although I had hoped to get some quilt blocks sewn today."

"I have an idea." Tasha poked Evan in the arm. "What if we take the kids?"

"Take the kids where?" Vera glanced curiously at Evan. She'd met him only once, but he seemed like a nice young man. Still, it was surprising to see him here with Tasha. Were they an item?

"That's a great idea," he said. "We're going to get Christmas trees."

"In fact, I wanted to get one for you," Tasha told Vera. "If you don't mind."

"Christmas trees!" Fiona exclaimed, popping her head around Vera's legs. "Can we get one too?"

"Of course you can," Evan told her.

"Well, as long as you ask your parents," Vera warned.

Evan pointed to Vera's newspaper sitting on the bench by her door. "According to the *Post*, today is the Christmas parade too. Maybe we should take that in first?"

"Brilliant!" Tasha wrapped an arm around Fiona. "I bet you kids would like to see the Christmas parade."

Suddenly all three of the children were leaping about, eager to get a Christmas tree and to see the Christmas parade, but Vera was uncertain. "You really need to talk to their parents," she told Tasha.

"Right." Tasha took the other poinsettia from Evan. "You and the kids stay here while I go ask permission, okay?"

Evan agreed and Tasha took off. Vera wasn't sure what Kerry and Josh would think about their three kids being swept away for a good part of the day, but when Tasha got back, carrying three jackets, it seemed the plan was set.

"Have fun," Vera said as they made their noisy mass exodus. "And please don't get me a very big tree," she called down the hallway. "I haven't much space in here." She closed her door with a relieved sigh. As much as she enjoyed those children, having some quiet time was a big relief.

* * *

They got to Main Street just in time to find places to watch the Christmas parade, but when Tasha noticed other children all bundled up in hats and mittens and warm winter coats, she felt bad for the Albrights. It was frosty cold today, and their thin coats couldn't possibly be keeping them warm enough. She'd already wrapped her scarf around Fiona and given Maureen her hat, but by the time Santa Claus came in his sleigh, pulled by Clydesdales for the grand finale, she could tell the children were chilled.

"Let's get you into the car to get you warmed up," she told the kids.

After they were all in the SUV with the heater running full blast, with the children in the back seat trading candy they'd gathered from the parade, Tasha voiced her concern to Evan. "I don't think their jackets are warm enough to go to the tree farm."

"You're probably right." He frowned as he waited for the sluggish parade traffic to get moving. He tapped the steering wheel with his gloved hands. "But I have an idea."

"What?" Tasha studied him.

"Theo is a friend of mine." He put on his turn signal and edged the car onto a side street.

"Theo?"

"She owns a very cool thrift store just a few blocks from here."

"Theodora's Threads?" Tasha asked, her interest piqued.

He nodded. "Yep. Let's go see if she carries kids' clothes."

"I've been in her shop," Tasha told him. "It's really nice, and I'm pretty sure there's a kids' section."

"Great," he said. "We're on our way."

A few minutes later Tasha spotted Theo's up ahead, and soon Evan was searching for a parking space.

"We're going to do a quick bit of shopping." Tasha explained the plan to get some warmer coats to the children. "So you kids won't freeze your tails off at the Christmas tree farm."

"But we don't have money for new coats," Nolan said in a tone laced with concern.

"Don't worry about that," Evan assured him. "My friend owns this place, and they have some special deals."

Before long, all five of them were wandering through the attractive little thrift shop. "Hello there." A tall redheaded woman came over to hug Evan. "Haven't seen you for a while, Evan. What's up?"

"Hey, Theo." He grinned. "Looking good."

Theo tossed a curious glance toward Tasha and the kids. "Got yourself a family now?" she teased.

Evan laughed. "Just for the day." He politely introduced her to Tasha and the kids. Then Tasha explained how the Albrights had relocated here from Arizona. "Naturally, they're not used to our cold weather, so they need some warm winter wear."

"Well, you've come to the right place." Theo stretched her arms out wide. "I got a bunch of winter things in recently. Seems like everyone was closet cleaning for Christmas. I haven't had time to sort it yet." She led them to the kids' section. "Go ahead and look here then go into the back room if you want to dig around a little more." She nudged Evan with her elbow. "In fact, I'll make you a real good deal on the stuff I haven't unloaded yet."

"Why don't we start there?" Tasha said.

"Fine with me." Theo tipped her head to Evan. "You know your way around here. Why don't you take them back? The boxes are by the big sorting table."

As Theo returned to the front of the shop, Evan guided Tasha and the kids through a door that led into a messy back room. "I know my way around here because I helped Theo when she first got this place. I actually put together a bunch of the shelving units out there." He winced. "At least, I hope they're still together. I'm not known for being very handy, but I am good at helping with her bookkeeping."

Just like Theo said, there were several heaping boxes on a folding table. "Well, I guess we just dig in," Tasha told the kids. "How about if we remove the items one by one, then kind of sort them out on the table for Theo?"

"Like we're helping her?" Maureen pulled out a navy-blue parka. "Hey, Nolan, this looks like your size."

He eagerly reached for the parka. "My friend Ryan at school has a coat like this."

"Try it on," Evan said to him.

It took a lot of sorting and trying on items, but eventually they found a warm winter coat for each of the kids. They were just taking their selections out to the front of the store when Theo met them with an armload of hats and mittens. "Anyone need any of these things? I'm offering a Christmas Parade Day half-off sale on all winter wear today."

By the time they left the shop, all three kids were well outfitted for the colder weather. Tasha tried to shove money at him, but Evan had insisted on paying for everything. And when she saw the total, which was incredibly reasonable, she couldn't help but be grateful to Theo. Next time she shopped there, which would probably be soon, Tasha would be sure to express her appreciation.

"It's nearly noon," Tasha whispered to Evan as he drove. "I wonder if we should get the kids some lunch or—"

"We'll have lunch at the tree farm," he told her with a twinkle in his eyes.

"Really?" She bobbed her head. "That should be interesting."

As it turned out, it was interesting. And fun. The tree farm had a huge cast-iron pot of chili cooking on an open fire, as well as hot dogs and hot cocoa and cookies. What more could a kid want? After lunch, they climbed onto a horse-drawn wagon and were taken out to the edge of the tree farm.

"You find the ones that suit you," the farmer told them, "and put them tags I gave you on your trees and set 'em by this road. In about an hour, I'll come back by with the wagon to collect 'em all and take 'em back to the parking lot. You can ride with the trees if there's room. Or else just walk back and get yourself some more cocoa and cookies while you wait."

So for the next hour, they walked and looked and eventually selected four trees. A small one for Vera, a mid-sized one for the flower shop, a fairly tall one for the Albrights, and an enormous one for Evan's house.

"Is your house really big enough for this tree?" Nolan asked Evan as he helped him carry it to the road.

"Yep. My dad always chose a fourteen-foot tree, and it went nearly to the ceiling in our living room."

"Wow." Maureen's eyes grew wide. "That's super tall."

"I've seen it," Fiona told her siblings with importance. "The living room in Evan and Eleanor's house is bigger than our whole house all put together."

"That's big," Nolan said.

"Well, I don't see the wagon yet." Evan looked down the

dirt road. "Should we go ahead and trek back to the barn on foot?"

The kids all decided to walk back and get more cocoa and cookies, but they hadn't gotten very far before Fiona's feet started dragging. "Looks like someone needs a ride." Evan swooped her up onto his shoulders. "How's that?"

"Giddyap," she said with renewed enthusiasm. And just like that, he took off in a lively trot, making her giggle hysterically as she yelled "whoa—whoa!" But he continued bouncing along, making the other two laugh as they ran to catch up with him. For a moment, Tasha just stood there watching the four of them frolic. Then she pulled out her phone and took some candid shots, but as she put it away, she knew she didn't need a photo to remind her of this moment. It was indelibly printed in her head. In fact, it seemed the whole day was. As she walked toward them, she wondered, *Will there ever be another day as perfect as this one?*

CHAPTER THIRTEEN

After dropping a tree behind the flower shop, Evan took Tasha and the kids back to the condo, and the five of them managed to get the two trees into the elevator and up to the right floor. Outside of Vera's door, Tasha thanked Evan and assured him that she and the kids could handle it from there. "That way you won't get in trouble for parking your SUV right out front."

"Good point." He checked his watch. "And I'll have enough time to get my mom's tree inside and clean myself up in time for tonight's gig."

"You have a gig tonight?"

He looked into her eyes. "It's nothing special. Just a Christmas party for a bank downtown. They're having it at the Marriott."

"Oh." She nodded.

"I was going to ask you to come," he said shyly. "Not that I think you want to be a groupie or anything, but if—"

"I'd love to come," she declared, hopefully not too quickly.

His face lit up. "Great. Can you be ready by six thirty?"

"You bet."

"I'll see you then." He beamed at her then took off toward the elevator.

"Is he your boyfriend?" Maureen asked Tasha.

"No," she answered quickly. "He's just my friend."

"He's Eleanor's son," Fiona said in a slightly spooky tone.

"Is that the wicked rich woman?" Nolan asked as he unlocked the door to their condo.

"Yes." Fiona nodded somberly. "She's kind of like a witch, isn't she, Tasha?"

Tasha suddenly felt guilty. Kneeling down to be eye level with Fiona, she spoke gently. "I know I said something mean like that before, Fifi. But I found out that Eleanor is just sad. And because she's sad, she acts mean."

Fiona's pale brows arched. "Then we should make her happy."

"Yes." Tasha hugged the little girl. "We should certainly try."

Nolan and Maureen were already dragging the tree into their condo. Both parents came over to supervise, listening as their excited children told them—all at once—about what they'd seen and done. Once the tree was upright, both Josh and Kerry stepped to the side to talk with Tasha privately.

"It was nice that you could take them," Kerry said. "I just haven't had the energy to do much yet."

"And I was exhausted from a long week and a late-night drive home," Josh said. "We really appreciated having a quiet day. Thanks."

"And the tree is lovely," Kerry told her.

"I should explain the coats." Tasha handed over the children's lightweight jackets. "My friend Evan has this friend who owns a thrift shop downtown. Theodora's Threads. Anyway, Theo was having a big sale today, and Evan insisted on treating the kids. I hope you don't mind."

Kerry grasped Tasha's hand with teary eyes. "That was so kind of him. Please, thank him for us."

"Yes," Josh said, agreeing. "Thank you both—so much."

"Well, we *all* had fun today," Tasha assured them. "Thank you for loaning us your kids. They're really great."

After she left the Albrights' home, Tasha rang Vera's bell. She opened the door with a large, quilted square in hand and tired eyes.

"That's pretty." Tasha carried the smaller tree into the room.

"So is that." Vera smiled at the tree. "Thank you." She led Tasha over to a small table where a large metal pot was waiting. "I hoped we could wedge the tree in there."

It took a bit of finagling, but the little tree was finally settled in and watered.

"Did you get lots of sewing done?" Tasha asked.

Vera nodded. "More than I expected. Having no interruptions helped."

"You look worn out, Vera. Maybe it's time to stop."

"I'm sure you're right." She yawned. "How about tea?"

"I'd love some." Tasha removed her coat.

"Great. You can tell me about your day with the children."

As Vera made tea, Tasha told her all about their adventures. "And Evan was so sweet. He's very good with kids."

"So, not like his mother, eh?" Vera's brows arched.

"Evan seems to be nothing like Eleanor." Tasha considered how to word what she really wanted to say. "In fact, I've learned some things about her through Evan." She sighed. "She's been through a lot, Vera."

"I suspected as much." Vera set two mugs of tea on the breakfast bar and sat down across from Tasha. "She seems like a troubled soul."

"Oh, she is." She shared about Eleanor's losses. "And within the same year. Can you imagine losing a child and a spouse?"

Vera just shook her head.

"Which is why she's so clingy with Evan. And why he moved back home. To help her through this."

Vera handed a mug to Tasha. "He's a good son."

"And a nice guy." Tasha sipped her tea.

"So . . . you and Evan?" She studied Tasha. "Does this mean you're dating?"

"Dating?" Tasha pictured high school kids making out in the hallways and shrugged. "Well, I'm not sure what you call it. But I must admit, I'm interested." She told Vera the plan to hear him and his band tonight. "In fact, I should probably go home and get cleaned up."

"Are you going to wear something pretty?" Vera's brows arched with interest.

Tasha grinned. "I'll do my best."

Vera patted her shoulder. "You have fun tonight, sweetie. After all you did for the Albright kids today, you deserve it."

Tasha shook her head. "All I did was have a really good time myself. Honestly, I can't remember ever having such a fun day. It was amazing."

Vera's eyes lit up. "Sounds like this thing with you and Evan might be part of that."

Tasha sighed as she tugged on her coat. "I don't know. I mean, if you knew my track record with men . . . Anyway, it's way too soon to tell." She reached for the doorknob. "But I'll enjoy what we have while we have it."

Vera's expression got slightly serious as she stood by the door. "Well, that's all you can do, sweetie. Take it one day at a time."

***

After Tasha left, Vera went over to admire her little tree. She didn't have any decorations or lights to put on it just yet, but its lovely color and shape and smell seemed enough for the time being. Much more than she'd expected a while back, when she'd given up on Christmas altogether. Looking out the window, she noticed Tasha downstairs, her scarf flapping in the wind as she waited at the crosswalk. Such an interesting, creative, free-spirited character.

As Tasha dashed across the street, Vera wondered, *What if this thing with Tasha and Evan does turn serious?* Unless she was mistaken, Tasha had seemed slightly starry-eyed today. What would Eleanor have to say about an unexpected romance? Besides the fact that she was probably overprotective of her son, Eleanor and the outspoken and strong-willed Tasha had already locked horns a number of times during quilting sessions. How much worse would it get if Eleanor discovered that Tasha was dating—or whatever they called it nowadays—her only son? Vera wasn't sure she wanted to find out. Her worried thoughts were interrupted by the sound of someone knocking on her door. She assumed it was Fiona since the little girl couldn't reach the doorbell. "Hello, little miss." Vera smiled at Fiona. "What can I do for you?"

"We got our tree put up by the window, but there's nothing to put on it."

"I see." Vera pointed to her own tree. "I'm in the same boat."

"You're in a boat?" Fiona frowned.

"Well, not a real boat. But I don't have any Christmas decorations myself." Vera rubbed her chin. "But I might use fabric scraps to make bows. And I'll have to get some white lights. I always liked white lights on a tree."

Fiona nodded but didn't look impressed. "So you don't have any real Christmas tree decorations?"

"Tell you what, Fiona. When I get lights for my tree, I'll get some for yours too."

Fiona perked up. "But can they be colors? Like pink and purple and orange?"

"Yes, they can be colored."

"When will you go get them?" Fiona asked.

Vera looked out the window. "Well, I don't like to drive after dark much, but it looks like I've got about an hour. I guess I could go now."

"I could help you carry things," Fiona offered with enthusiasm.

"Go ask your parents if it's okay," Vera told her. "And dress warm. I hear you got a new winter coat today.

Fiona nodded happily as she raced out the door. "It's purple. My favorite color."

Vera met Fiona in the hallway a few minutes later, and

soon they were on their way to the nearby BigMart where, instead of only getting lights like Vera had planned, they loaded up the cart with all kinds of Christmas ornaments and decorations. Oh, perhaps Vera was being extravagant, but the sparkle in Fiona's eyes and the thrill in her voice every time they found a new bright-colored item—well, if you can't be extravagant when you're almost five years old, when can you be?

* * *

Tasha really did feel like she was going on a date when she and Evan walked into the Marriott ballroom together. Wearing black pants and a gray turtleneck, Evan looked dignified, but not overdressed. After rummaging through her closet, Tasha had chosen a black velvet vintage dress with beadwork, and her favorite black booties. She could tell by Evan's expression that he approved of her outfit.

As he led her to a place to sit, he apologized for having to leave her on her own.

"Don't worry," she reassured him, "I love to people watch." And, really, she didn't mind. It was better than sitting at home with her mom and aunt. To her surprise, Evan's band was pretty decent. Oh, they might never make the big time, but for a small-town group of old high school buddies, they were not half bad.

"Are you bored out of your gourd yet?" Evan asked as he rejoined her during a break.

"I'm actually enjoying myself," she told him. "I like your band."

"And the people watching?"

She smiled. "Who knew bankers could be so interesting to spy on?"

"An accountant?" He chuckled.

"Oh, yeah, I suppose this is *your* sort of crowd," she teased.

"Not really. Some of them are pretty entertaining though. Like that middle-aged couple that's been rocking out to every song." He pointed to a couple a few tables away. "I'm impressed with their stamina."

"Me too. Some of the more dignified bankers are letting their hair down too. Of course, they've probably had too much Christmas cheer."

"Speaking of overimbibing." Evan nodded to a young couple having a heated argument. "Hope it's nothing serious."

"The holidays bring out the worst in some people," she said with a frown. She'd seen her own mother out of control more than once at Christmastime.

"Or the best." He smiled at her. "I had a really great time with you today, Tasha. I just wanted to say that. It was fun being with you and the Albright kids."

Her cheeks warmed. "I know! It was the best day ever. Thanks so much for hauling us around. My aunt loves the tree. I got it up and put lights on it. I plan to make some floral decorations for it on Monday when the new shipment gets in."

"That sounds pretty."

"What'd your mom think of your tree?"

He seemed to cringe then held up his hands in a surrender motion.

"She didn't like it, did she?" Tasha wasn't surprised. Just disappointed for Evan's sake.

"She actually seemed sort of shocked by it."

"It was a big tree." Tasha could imagine Eleanor's scowl of disapproval.

"Well, we always got big trees . . . before."

"So, did you put it up in the living room and everything?"

"I put it up, but it's not decorated. And if Mom has her way, it won't be." He shrugged. "Anyway, she said she won't lift a finger to decorate it. And I'm responsible for every needle it drops. I had to swear to get it out the day after Christmas." He rolled his eyes. "Happy holidays. Bah humbug."

"What if I helped you decorate it?" she said.

"You really want to?" His eyes lit up. "I mean, that'd be great, Tasha. If you're serious, I'd love your help. I'm not exactly the artsy one in the family." His smile faded. "That was, uh, Emily. She was really creative. And my dad was too, in his own way. Those two always took over decorating the tree. It was their tradition."

"You didn't mind being left out?"

"Not at all. I'd probably just have made a mess of it. And Mom's about as artistic as I am. We both knew to stay out of their way, but we always enjoyed their efforts when it was done."

"Well, I'd love to help you make your tree beautiful," Tasha said. "I don't like to blow my own horn, but I'm fairly creative myself."

His smile returned. "You on for tomorrow?"

She had just agreed to come over the following afternoon when his band members joined them. Introductions were made and they all visited for a while, but then the break was over. As Tasha absently watched the group performing and people dancing and drinking and fighting and making up, her mind was elsewhere. She imagined helping Evan decorate his gigantic tree. Hopefully, she hadn't taken on too much. What would Eleanor think of it? But Tasha was excited to see how beautiful they could make the giant tree. And who knew, maybe it would help to crack through Eleanor's ice-cold exterior . . . if that was even possible.

CHAPTER FOURTEEN

On Sunday Tasha was relieved to discover that Eleanor had gone out for groceries and that she and Evan had the house—and the tree decorating—to themselves. When she arrived, he took her to see the tree. Situated in front of the living room's bay window, it looked tall and majestic.

"Wow, it looks even bigger in here than it did at the tree farm," she told him.

"Yeah, I probably should've gotten a smaller one, but I kept thinking about Dad and Emily. They would both insist on one this big."

She put her hands on her hips and studied the towering tree. It would take a lot of decorations. "Well, I agree with them. It is majestic. We better get busy."

"The decorations are in a storage room on the second floor." He scratched his head. "At least, that's where they used to be. But for all I know, Mom might've gotten rid of them. She's gotten rid of a lot of stuff this past year."

"Oh, I hope not."

"Let's find out." He took her hand and led her toward the stairs. Before long, they were digging through a very crowded storage room.

"What is all this?" Tasha asked as Evan scooted a turquoise chair out of the way. "These don't really look like your mom's style of furnishings."

"No, not at all." He set a chrome floor lamp to one side. "This was Emily's stuff."

"Oh." Tasha felt a ripple of sadness.

"Dad and I moved it all up here after she died. That was before he got sick. I guess we just sort of forgot about it."

"There are some nice things in here." Tasha set a pretty throw pillow on a purplish sofa. "I like your sister's taste."

He shrugged. "Maybe you could use these things."

"I wish, but I don't have room for anything. Even the few furnishings I have are crammed into my aunt's attic. I pretend it's my studio sometimes, but mostly it's too hot or too cold up there."

"That's too bad." He lifted a box. "Eureka, I found it. At least one, anyway." He handed the cardboard box to her. "Go ahead and take this down, and I'll see if I can unearth a few more."

As she carried the box downstairs, she felt a wave of melancholy. This family and even this house . . . losing two family members within a year . . . well, she could almost feel the sadness seeping through the walls. Maybe the Christmas tree would help. She set the box down by the tree and opened it to find a wide assortment of ornaments. She was relieved to see there was no theme going on. Just random pieces with old-fashioned charm. This would be fun.

"I found all of them," Evan announced as he set a big box down. "Two more up there."

"Let's get 'em," she said with enthusiasm, before racing him up the stairs. Back in the storage room, she looked over the furnishings and boxes with a heavy heart. "Emily's things all seem fairly new." She pointed to a table lamp that still had its sales tag hanging from it.

"Yeah, Em was in her apartment only a couple months. She was still getting it all set up."

"Oh." Tasha picked up a faux fur pillow, then held it close like a stuffed bear. "Maybe you could return some of them to the stores."

"I wouldn't even know where she got them."

"Yeah, I guess that's not real practical." She took one of the boxes from him and started to go, then stopped. "You know who could really use some furniture, Evan?"

"Who?"

"The Albright family."

His eyes lit up. "That's right. I saw their condo yesterday. They're using lawn chairs and stuff. Not very cozy." He looked at the furnishings piled around them. "You think they'd want any of this?"

"I bet they'd love it. Especially the kids. I mean, all these bright, fun colors. Can you imagine the girls squealing over that plum-colored sofa?"

He chuckled. "Yeah, I can."

"Do you think your mother would agree?"

He lifted a box with a grunt. “I don’t see why not. She doesn’t need any of this stuff.”

“It would give her this spare room back.”

“Well, it’s not like she’s lacking spare rooms,” he said as he readjusted his grip on the box. “But as far as I know, she has no intention of ever downsizing.”

“Well, maybe you could ask her about it.” She waited for him to turn off the light and close the door. “Wouldn’t it be fun if the Albrights could have these things before Christmas?”

“That’d be awesome.”

They headed back to the living room and spent the next few hours decorating the tree. Evan hadn’t been exaggerating when he said he lacked creativity. But at least he was good at taking directions. Eventually they figured out a system where she would simply hand him an ornament and tell him where to hang it.

They were just finishing up when Evan cupped a hand to his ear. “I think that’s Mom. Probably putting away groceries.” Evan scrambled to pick up a couple of the nearly empty boxes. “I’ll get these upstairs. You put the rest of that away,” he whispered, gesturing toward the remaining decorations scattered across the room.

Tasha was gathering tissue paper and leftover bits and pieces, tossing them into the remaining two boxes, when she heard the loud click of footsteps approaching.

“What are you doing?” Eleanor yelled, exploding with anger. “What on earth have you done?”

Tasha turned to see Eleanor posed with hands on hips, staring down at her as if she’d broken into the house and stolen the family jewels.

"Uh, hi, Eleanor." Tasha stood up, dusting off her hands on her torn jeans. "How are you doing?"

"That is not the question. What do you think you are doing in here?"

"Decorating?" Tasha glanced over her shoulder, hoping Evan was on his way.

"Who gave you permission to come into my house? Let alone to decorate my tree?" Eleanor's face flushed. She shook her finger at the tree, as if it, too, was responsible for ruining her day.

"Mom!" Evan jogged into the living room, stopping only when he was by Tasha's side. "I'm the one who invited Tasha to—"

"I turn my back for five minutes and you take over my home?" She scowled at Evan.

"Wow, Mom. That's kinda harsh. I mean, I thought this was my home too."

"You *knew* I didn't want this—this tree!" She waved her hands all around. "And this mess!"

"You said the tree could stay up until Christmas," he protested. "I promised to clean up after it. I was just getting rid of these boxes and—"

"You have absolutely no respect for me or for my home." She glared at Tasha as if the words were meant for her.

"We were hoping you'd like it," Tasha said firmly. "We worked hard to make it pretty just for you."

Eleanor shook her head. "You mean for yourselves. You did this for yourselves. Not for me." She turned to her son with a pained expression. "Evan, you of all people know that seeing this tree only dredges up sad memories, reminds me of our loss. Can't you understand that? Your father and your sister are *gone*. This was their—"

"Oh, Mom." Evan went over and put an arm around her. "We hoped it would remind you of happier times and—"

"All it reminds me of is that they are gone. Never spending another Christmas here. It's like being stabbed in the back. Insult to injury." She shrugged off his arm, turned around, and stormed off.

"Wow." Tasha shook her head. "I'm so sorry, Evan."

His fists were clenched, and his expression was stony. "I don't understand her. It's like the whole world should be dead just because Dad and Emily aren't here."

Tasha could see tears forming in his eyes. "Oh, Evan." She rushed over and threw her arms around him and, hoping to comfort him, she held him close as he cried. Part of her worried that Eleanor might return and throw an even worse fit to see them embracing like this, but another part wished she would. Eleanor needed to see what she'd done to her son. Her only son!

"I'm sorry about that." Evan stepped away, wiping his wet face with his hands. "I'm not usually such a sissy."

Tasha shook her head. "There's nothing sissy about a man crying." She reached over to touch his arm. "In fact, I respect you even more for it."

He looked dubious. "Really?"

"Really and truly." She bent down to finish picking up the remaining decorations, then carefully placed them in the boxes in an attempt to hide her own misty eyes. Funny that she gave him permission to cry but denied it to herself. "We should get this put away." She cleared her throat.

"Maybe your mom will cheer up if it doesn't look so messy in here."

"I doubt it." But he helped anyway.

After they got the boxes stowed away and were back in the living room, Evan reached for the extension cord plug. "Want to see it lit up?" He smiled, though his eyes still looked troubled. They'd checked the string lights before draping them over the tree but had agreed not to turn it on until all the decorations were in place.

"Think your mom will get mad?"

He shrugged. "No madder than she was already." He squatted to plug in the lights. "Ready?"

"If you are." Tasha stepped back for a better viewpoint, watching as the lights came on. "Oh, it's beautiful, Evan. I'm so glad you have multicolored lights. Some people prefer all one color. That can be pretty, but these colorful lights are so cheerful. And with the ornaments, it's stupendous!"

Evan brightened. "Emily always insisted on multicolored lights. Mom wanted to go all white one year, but Emily convinced her that was too cold and formal."

Tasha sighed. "I agree with Emily."

Evan sighed as well. "This tree really looks like Emily and Dad decorated it." He stepped back by Tasha and gazed up with appreciation. "It's like they participated somehow."

"Maybe they did." Tasha felt a warm shiver course through her. "It's too bad your mom wasn't happily reminded of them. Or maybe it's just too soon."

"I don't know." Evan slipped his arm around her, pulling her closer to him. "But I love it. Thanks for helping, Tasha. Sorry Mom had to rain on our parade."

"It's okay. We probably forced too much on her." She almost added that Eleanor might feel the same way about Tasha, especially since she didn't seem to approve of his friendship with her.

"Maybe."

They both heard her footsteps and Tasha pulled away from his embrace and turned to see Eleanor approaching with a hard-to-read expression. At least she wasn't armed and dangerous. Just the same, Tasha braced herself.

"Well, I suppose I should apologize." Eleanor's tone was aggravated but controlled. Perhaps she had transitioned into therapist mode. "It wasn't right for me to say those things. You kids didn't do this to anger me. I know that." She sat down on the sofa, slumping her shoulders as her eyes roved over the tree. "I must admit, it looks rather nice."

Evan went to sit down beside his mother, then took her hand. "We did it to make you happy, Mom. We hoped you'd like it. And we were just saying how it felt like Dad and Emily helped us somehow. Sort of like they were watching on, you know? Can't you try to enjoy it just a little? For their sake?"

Eleanor nodded, her eyes watery. "Yes, yes . . . I can try. I can't promise more than that. But I can try."

Tasha was torn. Her self-preservation half wanted to make a run for safety while Eleanor was still cooled off, but her more adventurous side hoped for a real connection. "I was just telling Evan how much I love these cheerful colored lights and all your beautiful decorations, Eleanor. It's such a lovely family tree."

"Yes, Emily loved the colored lights too."

"I wish I'd known Emily." Tasha shoved her hands into her jeans pockets. "I'm sure I would've liked her."

"And she would've liked you," Evan assured her.

Tasha glanced toward the foyer. "Well, I should probably go. Thanks for letting me help, Evan. I never decorated such a big tree before."

"Rolland always insisted on a big tree," Eleanor said in an absentminded way. "He always cleaned up the needles for me. He was so good about that." She looked at Evan with more clarity. "Just like you'll do, young man."

"Yes, Mom." Evan grinned at Tasha.

Tasha took a step toward the foyer. "Well, I should—"

"Wait, before you leave," Evan interrupted her, then turned to his mother. "Tasha and I got this great idea, Mom." His eyes glistened hopefully as he explained about the Albrights' rickety lawn chairs and lack of furnishings. "They could really use Emily's things. And the kids would love the bright colors and—"

"No." Eleanor shrugged off his hand and stood. "It's one thing for you to plot against me by sneaking this gargantuan tree into my house, but do not start giving away your sister's things, Evan."

"But we don't need them and—"

"How do you *know* that?" She shook her finger at him like he was a child. "Maybe *I* need them! Did you ever ask yourself that?"

"No, but I thought—"

"You *didn't* think. That's the problem." She glared at Tasha. "With both of you. You're not thinking. Neither of you. Not thinking of anyone or anything but yourselves." She waved her hands as if to dismiss them, then stomped off.

"I guess I shouldn't have done that." Evan sighed. "I just hoped she was softening up."

"Don't worry about it." Tasha kept her tone light. "At least she was better about the tree. Maybe just take it slowly, Evan. She's obviously hurting. And you know what they say, hurt people hurt people."

He got off the couch and closed the space between them. "So I've heard, but I know you've been hurt, Tasha. Probably even more than you've said. I don't see you hurting anyone." He wrapped his arms around her, and she felt herself melting into his embrace.

"Well, sometimes I want to lash out," she whispered. She didn't want to admit how many times she'd wanted to go after Eleanor for her crankiness. "But then I try to remember someone else . . . someone who got hurt . . . really badly . . . for me."

"Huh?" Evan held her back to look at her face, but he seemed confused. "Who was that? Not your ex."

Tasha hadn't told him much about her ex on that first coffee date but was surprised his thoughts went straight there. She simply shook her head and went over to the tree, pointing to a mini manger scene dangling from a sturdy bough. "I mean the one behind our Christmas celebration—the reason for the season. You know?"

"Oh, yeah." He came over to study the ornament. "Thanks for the reminder. I guess I needed that."

She turned to him and, gently tugging him down to her level, kissed him. On the cheek. "Thanks, Evan. For everything." And before he could respond beyond looking completely surprised, she scurried off, snatched up her coat, and made her exit. As she walked through the crisp, cool air, she felt her head clear a bit. It was like a warning message going through her mind. *Be careful. You're in the danger zone again.*

She knew Evan wasn't dangerous. That wasn't it. He was just a very sweet albeit somewhat naive guy. But a romance with him might turn into a minefield of heartache. Because of Eleanor. She'd felt the older woman's judgment right from the start. Although Tasha had tried to convince herself she was just a crank, she knew Eleanor targeted Tasha more than Beverly and Vera.

Maybe Tasha deserved some of her criticism for being outspoken and opinionated, but beneath that she'd wondered . . . was it something more? Was it because Tasha hadn't grown up with Evan's privileges? Because she didn't have a fancy education? Or because she was divorced? Those were things she couldn't change. And if Eleanor was that narrow-minded, Tasha wanted nothing more to do with the Rasmussen world. She had no room in her life for that kind of pain.

CHAPTER FIFTEEN

Despite a few more quarrels over silly things like snacks and music selections and whose turn it was to iron, all four women had been working hard on the complicated Nordic Star pattern. But it was their last week before Christmas, and it would take everyone doing their part just to get the quilt top finished.

To Vera's relief, the women worked quietly and efficiently for a few days—with minimal squabbling. Beverly brought no treats to rile Eleanor or distract the others. And Tasha, quieter than usual, had taken over Vera's sewing machine and produced fine-looking quilt blocks. Of the three quilting recruits, Tasha was definitely the most talented and, seeing the end of the project in sight, Vera was extremely grateful for the young woman.

So far, the week had been all work and no play. Even Fiona seemed to understand the seriousness of the sewing mission as she curled up on a fuzzy beanbag chair that Evan had sweetly brought in for her on Monday. He'd also taped a sign above it that read FIONA'S CORNER. Not that his mother liked it. He'd even set up a clunky old TV and VCR system for her, as well as a basket of old VHS tapes. Fiona was happy as a clam.

Finally, it was the last day for the quilters to meet. To celebrate, Beverly had brought a pretty plate of dark chocolate walnut fudge and some tree-shaped sugar cookies that she'd frosted in green and decorated with colorful sprinkles. Naturally Eleanor disapproved.

"I'm sorry to offend you," Beverly told their hostess as she laid out festive paper plates, napkins, and a thermos of delicious-smelling coffee, "but I thought we needed something special to commemorate finishing our quilt."

"It's not finished *yet*," Eleanor said sharply.

"It won't be long," Vera said in a soothing tone, as she placed a hand on Eleanor's shoulder. "At least the top should be completely done today." She unfolded a strip of blocks that she'd stitched together the day before. "Isn't it looking beautiful!"

Tasha ran a hand over the colorful section. "I love these colors together. The contrasts are so rich—and perfect for any season."

"Oh, it's just gorgeous," Beverly gushed. "Now I want to make one exactly like it for myself."

"I'll still have to add the batting and attach it to the backing," Vera said. "But that won't take too long, thanks to my long arm quilting machine. It does most of the work for me. Although it takes supervision. But I plan to devote myself to it throughout next week. It'll easily be done before Christmas."

Fiona had already admired the pretty quilt strip and was now eagerly eyeing the plate of sweets.

Vera smiled at her. "Okay, Fiona, you can have some now if you promise to eat the healthy snacks I packed for you later." Fiona happily agreed, then wrapped up her treats and toted them back to her little corner. Now the expert on old video systems, she popped in a VHS tape and settled in.

"I can't believe you're letting that child consume so much sugar." Eleanor frowned at Vera, then turned to Beverly. "And here I'd hoped you'd changed your ways, but I see I'm wrong."

"Changed my ways?" Beverly chuckled as she handed paper plates to Tasha and Vera. "I just have to tell you girls how much fun I had yesterday morning." She directed this to Vera and Tasha. "I visited the Albright home. Remember, I wanted to help Kerry set up her kitchen for baking? I have way too many baking pans and things, and she had practically nothing. Did you know she worked in a bakery in Dublin before she was married? She was the lead baker."

"Interesting." Vera took a bite of some fudge. "Oh, Beverly this is yummy!"

"Kerry and I made it together. It's my secret recipe, but I shared it with her. Tomorrow morning she's going to teach me how to make scones."

"What a great idea." Tasha bit into a cookie.

Beverly pointed to Vera. "She suggested it." She lowered her voice, then glanced toward Fiona, who looked totally absorbed in an old Christmas movie. "I had no idea. Oh my, that poor little family. Do you know that they moved here with practically nothing but the clothes on their backs? They used what money they had to get beds for everyone. The rest is practically all lawn furniture."

"I know." Tasha nodded solemnly.

"I wish I'd met them before I moved from my big house," Vera said. "I got rid of so many nice things that they could've used."

Eleanor loudly cleared her throat as she sat down in front of her machine. "Well, ladies, if we want to finish this quilt, shouldn't we get busy? Vera, do you have some system in mind for putting these blocks together?"

Still munching on a sugar cookie, Vera outlined her plan for stitching blocks into strips and connecting them, explaining who would do what and how it should work. "You're all doing such an excellent job sewing, I'll manage just the ironing today."

"You'll have plenty of sewing to do when you attach and quilt the back," Tasha reminded her. "By the way, I'd love to see how that's done."

"Come on over next week and I'll show you how to run the long arm machine," Vera told her.

Before long, they were all busily working again and, despite Eleanor's wet blanket treatment of Beverly, there seemed to be almost a cheerful spirit in the air. Tasha played a nice selection of Christmas music on her phone, and all the machines whirred busily. Vera felt almost happy as she steamed seams open—or maybe it was simply relief that their challenging project was finally coming to an end. Although she would miss the company of Beverly and Tasha, she would not regret parting ways with Eleanor. Besides, she knew she'd continue her friendship with Tasha, and Beverly, too, since she'd begun attending her church.

"I'm going to start delivering Christmas cookie plates this weekend," Beverly said to the group. "All year long I collect pretty plates from thrift shops and garage sales. I try to get ones that fit the personalities of my friends and neighbors and then I load them with goodies. It's so much fun! Naturally, I plan to bring you girls a plate too. Well, not everyone. Don't you worry, Eleanor." Beverly chuckled. "Although I might try to sneak something to that nice young man who lives in your basement."

Eleanor harrumphed as she stood up, brushing thread trimmings from her tweed pants. "I suppose I can't stop you from poisoning my son."

"Oh, Eleanor." Vera couldn't stop herself from cutting in. "A few sweets at Christmastime are not poison. Surely, you know that."

"I do know that white sugar is more addictive than cocaine." Eleanor put her hands on her hips.

For a moment the room was quiet except for the Christmas music, then Beverly let out a loud whoop of laughter. "You can't be serious!"

"I'm dead serious." Eleanor raised her voice. "I've read scientific studies that have been performed on rats. Sugar affects the brain as much as any addictive drug. It causes the same druglike effects such as bingeing, craving, and withdrawal. Rats that were given white sugar were—"

"Look, Eleanor," Vera said gently but firmly, "none of us are saying sugar should be consumed on a daily basis, but good grief, it's Christmastime. Can't you just lighten up a little?"

"No!" Eleanor yelled. "I cannot lighten up, thank you very much. This is my home, and if I prefer not to have Beverly dealing her drugs to my own son, I should have a right to say so."

"Well!" Now Beverly stood, facing Eleanor with a flushed face. "If you want me to leave, I will."

"Oh, really, ladies"—Tasha stood as well, but her expression remained calm—"are we really fighting over cookies? Seriously? I mean, we're creating this beautiful—"

Eleanor spun on Tasha. "Are you saying I don't have the right to ban dangerous drugs from my home?"

"Well, I'm just saying—"

"I don't want to hear what you're saying. I'm sick to death of everyone defending Beverly and her sugary sweets." Eleanor threw her hands in the air and let out a loud sigh.

Vera noticed that Fiona had left her corner and was watching this ridiculous spectacle with widened eyes. Vera was about to say something, but Fiona spoke up first.

"Maybe Mrs. Rasmussen needs a dentist."

"What?" Tasha tilted her head to one side.

"Like the bottom mole snowman."

Eleanor scowled at Fiona. "What on earth are you babbling about?"

"You're like the bottom mole snowman," Fiona bravely explained to her.

"What is a *bottom mole* snowman?" Eleanor crossed her arms.

"Bumble is the bottom mole snowman. He had a bad

tooth that made him growl at everyone." Fiona pointed at Eleanor. "Maybe you do too."

Suddenly Beverly burst into giggles. "She was watching that old Rudolph movie. Do you mean the *abominable* snowman, honey?"

"Yeah. He was real mean until the elf dentist pulled his bad tooth, then Bumble was real nice."

Vera was trying not to giggle. "I remember that movie."

"The *bottom mole* snowman." Tasha laughed loudly. "That's a good one." Suddenly they were all laughing. Everyone except Eleanor. Her expression was hard to read—perhaps more sad than angry now. Then Vera noticed that Fiona wasn't laughing either. With a serious expression, the little girl went over to Eleanor and reached up to take her hand.

"I didn't mean to hurt you, Mrs. Rasmussen. You're not really a bottom mole snowman. You just need a friend." Fiona smiled bravely. "I'll be your friend. And if you don't want me to eat cookies at your house anymore, I won't."

"Oh . . ." Eleanor shook her head with pursed lips. "That's not necessary."

The room grew quiet again, except for Tasha's phone, which was now playing an instrumental version of "Little Drummer Boy." Vera thought the old tune was rather apropos.

"Please, excuse me," Eleanor said quietly. "I have a severe headache and need to lie down."

After she left, Fiona turned to Vera. "Is a headache like a toothache? Like the bottom mole snowman had?"

"Yes." Vera patted Fiona's blond head. "Something like that, sweetie."

"More than you probably know," Tasha said.

Beverly nodded. "And a little child shall lead them . . ."

With more sewing to finish, the three of them went back to work and Fiona returned to her corner. No one spoke for a while. The sound of machines whirring and music playing filled the room. After about an hour, they took a break.

"As much as I've enjoyed learning to quilt, I'm so glad this is our last day up here," Tasha confessed as she munched on a cookie.

"Me too," Beverly agreed.

"I'm sure Eleanor is eager to get us out of her hair too," Vera said.

They returned to work, and after another hour, the quilt top was all in one piece. Vera shook it out so they could see it. "Since the iron is still hot, I think I'll go ahead and press out these seams. You two can go ahead and leave if you want."

Beverly and Tasha packed up their things and eventually left, but Vera continued working, ironing the quilt top, taking her time to get it just right, and pausing to cut a few missed threads. She was just finishing up when Fiona called out to tell Vera her cell phone was ringing.

To Vera's surprise, it was her son on the other end. Worried something might be wrong, she answered quickly. "Bennett? How are you?"

"Well, we're just driving into Fairview, Mom. Lola and I decided to come through here on our way to Boise. Do you have time to meet us for a late lunch?"

"Of course. I'd love to see you both!"

"How about Green Trees? Lola found the place on her phone, and it's got good reviews. We're only five minutes from it right now. Could you meet us there? We don't have long, but we'd love to see you."

"I'll leave now." She was already folding the quilt top. "I should be there in about ten minutes. That is, if traffic's not bad."

"Great. See you soon."

As she slid her phone into her bag, she remembered she still needed to pack up her sewing things. And then there was Fiona. She needed to drop her at home. Ten minutes was not realistic.

"You're still here?" Eleanor stood in the doorway, looking on with a slightly weary expression. "I thought everyone had gone."

"No. Tasha and Beverly left. We did finish the quilt top though." She nodded to where she'd laid it on the table. "Fiona and I are about to leave too." As Vera unplugged the iron and started to gather her things, she explained about Bennett's unexpected visit. "I said ten minutes, but I still need to pack things up and take Fiona home and—"

"Let me do that for you."

Vera blinked in surprise. "Really?"

"Yes." Eleanor came into the room to look at the quilt top. "It's the least I can do. You go meet your son, Vera." She glanced at Fiona. "You'll help me clean up, won't you, Fiona? Since we're friends now?"

Fiona smiled. "I'll help you."

"Just leave everything to me. I'll deliver it to your condo later today."

Vera didn't know what to say, but she didn't argue as she grabbed her purse and thanked Eleanor. As she hurried down the stairs, she wondered, *Has the bottom mole snowman gotten better somehow?* She hoped so. Otherwise, she should probably be worried for Fiona's sake. But for some reason, she wasn't.

* * *

Eleanor had never been very good with children. Not even her own. That was always Rolland's territory. But something about Fiona seemed different from other children. Certainly, she was intelligent, but more than that, it seemed the little girl had an old soul. Even as she helped Eleanor pack up Vera's sewing things, she was surprised she knew where to put things. Perhaps she'd helped Vera before.

Somehow this outspoken, precocious child had gotten through to Eleanor when she'd accused her of being a bottom mole snowman. Funny how something so silly and childish had cut right through Eleanor's frosty heart. But it had. Eleanor had no doubts that she'd acquired a very frosty heart in the last couple of years.

"Well, I think we got everything," Eleanor finally said. "Let's take one load downstairs and I will bring the other things later. After all, Vera won't even be home for a while."

"Will she be gone for the day?" Fiona asked as they trudged down the stairs.

"Oh, I don't know." Eleanor set a sewing case on the foyer bench. "Maybe."

Fiona's face seemed to crumble as tears filled her eyes.

"It's nothing to cry about," Eleanor gently scolded. "You can see her tomorrow, can't you?"

"But we were s'posed to make my costume."

"Costume?"

"For the Christmas play at church. It's tomorrow. Vera was going to make it."

"Oh." Eleanor reached for Fiona's parka. "What kind of costume were you going to make?"

"I'm an angel." Fiona wiped her nose with her sweatshirt sleeve.

"An angel?" Eleanor laid the parka on the bench and rubbed her chin. "What if I had an angel costume you could use?"

Fiona's blue eyes grew huge. "*You* have an angel costume?"

Eleanor nodded. "As a matter of fact, I do."

"Really?" Fiona grabbed her hand. "Is it my size?"

"Let's go find out." Eleanor led Fiona back up the stairs, then opened the door to the room that had once been Emily's. Although she'd changed it into a guest room when Emily was in college, she'd kept her old cedar chest in there. It was filled with sweet memorabilia from her little girl's childhood. She hadn't opened it in years. Not even after Emily had died.

"This is a pretty room," Fiona said cheerfully as they went inside.

As Eleanor slowly lifted the lid of the chest, the pungent smell of cedar wafted up, reminding her of when her own grandmother had given the chest to her as a girl. She pulled a chair over and carefully removed a box containing several old dolls and another box with a slightly chipped china tea set. The lump in her throat grew harder as she lifted out a floral print Easter dress from when Emily was eight. Eleanor had sewn it herself.

"That's so pretty," Fiona said.

Eleanor nodded, setting the dress aside. "Here it is." She removed a Christmassy box that was slightly crushed and laid it on the floor. "Go ahead, open it."

Fiona knelt by the box, then reverently lifted the lid. "Oh my!" She clasped her hands in front of her as if afraid to touch what was inside. "It's so beautiful!"

Eleanor lifted out a shimmering white frock. Years ago, she'd searched every fabric store in town to find the white iridescent fabric. She fingered the gold cording fondly, remembering how long it had taken to hand-stitch it around all the edges. She held the gown up to Fiona. "Looks like a perfect fit. My little Emily was five years old when she wore it in a Christmas pageant."

"I'm almost five," Fiona said, pointing a finger toward her chest.

Eleanor took out the wings, also trimmed with gold braid that was sewn to the wires. They were a little bent out of shape, but she was pretty sure they could be fixed. Finally, she picked up the gold-trimmed halo and placed it on the girl's blond head. "You'll make a very sweet angel, Fiona."

Fiona threw her arms around Eleanor, hugging her tightly with childlike enthusiasm. To Eleanor's relief, the happy girl couldn't see the tears streaming down her cheeks as she hugged the little angel back.

CHAPTER SIXTEEN

Eleanor knew where the Albrights lived but had never been inside their home. Fiona proudly led the way to their door and when her mother opened it, the little girl insisted that Eleanor come inside.

"I don't want to intrude," Eleanor told Mrs. Albright, explaining why she'd brought Fiona home.

"Look what Mrs. Rasmussen gave me!" Fiona thrust the worn Christmas box toward her mother.

"It's a costume for the church pageant." Eleanor remained in the doorway. "My little girl wore it many years ago."

"It's the most beautiful angel costume in the whole wide world!" Fiona was dancing with joy. "Can I try it on now, Mama?"

"After your nap," Mrs. Albright said firmly.

"Okay!" Still clutching the box, Fiona dashed off. "I'm gonna sleep fast!"

"That was very kind of you, Mrs. Rasmussen." Mrs. Albright made what seemed like a weary, or perhaps sad, smile.

"Please, call me Eleanor." She studied the attractive woman, wondering what was troubling her. Something definitely seemed wrong. "Vera had planned to make Fiona's costume, but she's been, uh, very busy . . . and today I remembered my daughter's old costume." Eleanor couldn't help but notice the room behind Mrs. Albright. Evan had not exaggerated about how sparse and pathetic it seemed. Perhaps that was what was bothering the woman.

"Vera's been a jewel helping me out like she's done. I shall never be able to repay her for her kindness." Mrs. Albright sighed. "Goodness, where are my manners? Please, come in."

Eleanor was torn. Part of her wanted to turn the other way, another part—perhaps the old counselor in her—wondered what was troubling this young mother.

"I just put on the kettle," Mrs. Albright told her. "Do you like tea?"

"I would love a cup of tea," Eleanor admitted. "Thank you, Mrs. Albright."

"Please, call me Kerry." She led the way to the little kitchen, pointing to the breakfast bar. "Have yourself a seat and rest your weary bones."

Eleanor pulled out a rickety metal stool and cautiously perched. "This is a nice condo unit." She took in the stainless steel appliances and granite countertop in the tidy kitchen.

"Yes, I suppose it's nice enough. Not ideal for children, and not very thrifty for the pocketbook, but 'twas all we could find on such short notice." She sighed as she swished hot water around to warm the teapot. A British custom, but something Eleanor did as well.

"Unfortunately we've been unable to furnish it. We left

Arizona in such a mad rush, we couldn't bring much. Not that we had much to bring, mind you." She dumped the warming water into the sink, then measured out some loose-leaf tea and poured it into the pot.

"Why did you leave in such a rush?" Eleanor gently asked.

"Oh, it all happened after Josh's mother passed. Josh is my husband, and you see, he and his older sister, Jessica, never got on too well. Jessica doesn't get on too well with anyone, including her dearly departed mother. But as soon as their mother passed, Jessica showed up." She paused to pour hot water into the teapot. "Mind you, Jessica never visited while her mother was suffering so . . . and while we took care of her. But Jessica showed up in time for the funeral—and the reading of the will. Josh's dear mother left everything she had to him, but Jessica and her lawyers immediately contested it.

"So now the whole works, including some of our own things, are all tied up with her lawyers and court and such. It's a mess." She set the teapot and cups on the counter and took a stool on the opposite side of Eleanor. "Josh needed to find work—and get away from his sister—so we came up here. Josh said Oregon was a wee bit like Ireland, but I'm not so sure about that. I do miss my Dublin at times."

"That must've been very hard on you. On all of you."

Kerry nodded as she poured the tea through a little sifter. "It was good to get the children away from it. There's such bitterness in the air down there. Even if we're poor up here, it's better than fighting with Jessica down there." She slid a cup toward Eleanor.

"I see your point." Eleanor sniffed the golden tea. It was not herbal, but it smelled lovely.

"Just when I thought I was getting on top of things, I had my appendicitis attack. And then an infection afterward. It's all just knocked me flat." She shook her head, then sipped her tea. "I suppose I was sitting here feeling sorry for myself just now, before you came in. I know I should be happy. I have so much to be thankful for—my children, my husband. But I feel a bit stuck, do you know?" She peered at Eleanor with dark, intense eyes. "I don't suppose you would."

But Eleanor slowly nodded. "As a matter of fact, I do know. I've been a bit stuck myself. And to be honest, I've been feeling sorry for myself lately."

"Whatever for?" Kerry looked keenly interested.

To her own amazement, Eleanor spilled the tale of her unbearable year—of losing her daughter and then her husband. "I think I've been angry at everyone," she confessed. "I thought I had a right to my grief and bitterness, and that it would simply run its course. But instead of getting better, I've only gotten worse."

Kerry listened with wide eyes and an intense expression as Eleanor shared how little Fiona had called her out on it today. "She called me the bottom mole snowman." Kerry looked shocked, but Eleanor quickly explained. Once they'd both had a good laugh over it, Kerry had tears streaming down her cheeks. Reaching for a paper napkin, she wiped them.

"Oh, I'm so sorry for your loss, Eleanor. So very, very sorry. Your story is much sadder than mine."

Eleanor felt her cheeks warming. "I can't believe I told you all that. I don't usually share so openly about personal things."

"Then I thank you." Kerry came around to the other side

of the breakfast bar to slip an arm around Eleanor's shoulders. She gave her a sideways squeeze. "I appreciate you trusting me with your story. To be honest, I've never shared my troubles with anyone either. I felt it was my burden to bear. I didn't want to trouble Josh . . . or worry the children. But for some reason I felt you'd understand."

"I do understand." Eleanor set down her teacup.

"Since I'm being honest, I'll confess that besides feeling sorry for myself, I was feeling guilty too." Kerry went over to where the Christmas tree stood in front of the window. It was the only truly cheery thing in their home. "It's almost Christmas, Eleanor, and here I am feeling like old Mr. Scrooge himself."

"I know exactly what you mean." Eleanor cringed to remember the fit she'd thrown over her own Christmas tree. "At least your tree is festive. It should lift your spirits."

"Yes. Thanks to your fine son and dear Tasha. And Vera too. She took Fiona to get the decorations. The children just love it." Kerry paused by a card table in the dining area, picking up a platter of Christmas tree cookies that looked very similar to the ones Beverly had brought to Eleanor's home that morning, only these were unfrosted. "Where are my manners? I should've offered a cookie with your tea."

Eleanor was about to reject the treat but stopped herself and picked one up. "Thank you." As she bit into the cookie, she was surprised at its taste. Instead of being overwhelmingly sugary sweet, like she'd imagined, it tasted like vanilla and butter with a hint of cinnamon. "This is really good." She took another bite.

"It's Beverly's recipe. They remind me of the shortbread

my mother used to make." Kerry nibbled on the point of a tree-shaped cookie. "Makes me think of home."

"Is your mother still in Ireland?" Eleanor asked.

Kerry shook her head. "She passed on years ago, before I was married."

"I am sorry."

"'Tis all right. I still got my dad." She smiled. "He's just retired. Living in Dublin with his brother's family." Her brow creased. "We'd hoped to have him join us by now. We planned to all be together this Christmastime. Down in Arizona. Josh's mother's house had plenty of room. Dad even got his passport last summer, and we'd promised to buy him a plane ticket. But then it all fell apart when Josh's mother passed . . . and we had to move so suddenly. The children were terribly disappointed."

Eleanor drew her eyebrows together. "That's too bad."

"Yeah. Family should be together at Christmas." Kerry sighed. "Will you have your family with you? I mean, other relatives and such?"

"It's just Evan and me." Eleanor pursed her lips as an idea began to formulate. "Unless you and your family would like to join us?"

Kerry perked up. "Join you?"

"Yes." Eleanor nodded eagerly. "We have a large, comfortable house. We'd love to have your family with us. Evan is quite fond of your children."

Kerry smiled. "And they love him. Him and Tasha. They couldn't stop talking about those two after getting the tree and all."

"And I'll invite Vera as well," Eleanor said. "She's alone for Christmas. People shouldn't be alone at Christmas."

"No, they shouldn't." Kerry clapped her hands together. "Oh, the children will be so happy to hear we've got plans."

Eleanor finished her tea and stood. "Well, I've got errands to run. I'll be in touch with you about the particulars for Christmas."

"Thank you for listening to me, Eleanor. I actually feel better now. Sort of hopeful." She smiled again. "You're a good listener."

Eleanor returned her smile and started toward the entrance. "Well, I used to be. I might need to work on it some."

"And I hope you'll come see Fiona in her Christmas pageant." Kerry followed her to the door.

"She made me promise I would," Eleanor admitted, "so I better be there."

Kerry opened her arms and fully embraced Eleanor, thanking her again for listening. The young woman's enthusiasm felt familiar. Perhaps it reminded Eleanor of Fiona. Or maybe her own sweet Emily. Or maybe it just felt like family.

* * *

Tasha remained out of sorts for the rest of Friday. Nothing about their little quilting group had ended in the way she'd hoped. Oh, sure, she'd learned a lot about quilting and was glad to have gained Vera and Beverly as friends, but the overall feeling was one of extreme disappointment. So much so that when Evan asked her to go out with him that evening, she feigned a headache—or was it real?

The next morning, working in the back room of the florist shop, her aunt questioned her about her gloomy demeanor. Tasha tried to brush it off, but Aunt Susan wouldn't let it go.

"It's that quilting bunch you've been hanging with. Those old ladies have messed with your mind," she teased. "You need to get away from it all, Tash. Why don't you come down to Cabo for Christmas with your mom and me? It's probably not too late to get a flight."

"Thanks, but I already told you and Mom, Christmas in Mexico doesn't appeal to me." Tasha stuck a red rose into the bouquet she'd been working on, then stood back to admire it.

"I think those old ladies gave you an aging lobotomy—like a weird sci-fi flick. It's like you've become one of them."

Tasha laughed, but it didn't feel genuine. "Maybe I'm just not into a *Cabo Christmas*. You should be glad—who else would keep your shop open while you're gone? Who knows, it could get busy this week." As if to make her point, the bell out front jingled.

"Good girl." Aunt Susan patted Tasha on the head. "Maybe next year, huh?"

Tasha just shrugged as her aunt left to help the customer, but moments later she returned with a strange twinkle in her eyes. "Speaking of the little old ladies, one of them wants to see you."

Thinking it was probably Vera, Tasha wiped her hands on her apron and went out. To her surprise and displeasure, it was Eleanor. Tasha braced herself for whatever was about to transpire—hopefully the woman wasn't about to read her the riot act regarding Evan. Tasha assumed Eleanor wanted her out of his life. Just the same she forced a smile as she politely greeted her.

"Oh, Tasha." Eleanor almost smiled. "Do you have a few minutes to talk?"

Tasha's shock instantly morphed into fear. "What's wrong? Did something happen to Evan?"

"No, no. Evan's just fine. But we could use your help. Are you working all day?"

"Just the morning." Bursting with curiosity, Tasha ignored her aunt's open stare as she led Eleanor to the back room. "What's going on?" she asked as she closed the door.

Suddenly Eleanor poured out her concerns for the Albright family, explaining how she'd gotten to know Kerry the day before. "She's such a dear girl. And you and Evan were right—that family desperately needs some decent furnishings. I want to help."

Tasha suppressed the urge to demand, *Who are you and what have you done with the real Eleanor Rasmussen?* Instead, she bit her tongue and just listened.

"Evan got a rental truck and a friend to help him move Emily's things," Eleanor quickly explained. "Since Vera's an interior designer, she's agreed to arrange the furnishings, but we must get the Albrights out first. It has to be a surprise. Well, mostly. Josh is in the loop. I wanted his permission. And, of course, he gave me Murphy's phone number."

"Huh?" Tasha's head was spinning. "Who is Murphy?"

Eleanor shook her head. "Never mind that right now. I'll explain later. Anyway, here's where you come in, Tasha. I want you to take the kids Christmas shopping, and maybe to a movie if you need to kill more time. Beverly will pick up Kerry to go bake at her house. We need everything wrapped up around five. Josh should be home by then. He's ordering pizza for their dinner before the Christmas pageant at the church." Eleanor was slightly out of breath by the time she finished.

Tasha slowly nodded. "So you've orchestrated this three-ring circus in order to furnish the Albrights' condo?"

"I know it sounds crazy, but I think it will work. Won't it be a wonderful surprise for them?"

"Yes." Tasha was catching Eleanor's enthusiasm now. "I'm happy to help."

Eleanor checked her watch. "I have an appointment with my travel agent to arrange things for Murphy. Then I've got a lot of shopping and errands to do, or I'd take the children myself." She paused to take a breath. "You can handle it, right?"

"Absolutely." Tasha removed her apron. "I'll be minding the shop by myself next week, so I might as well enjoy some time off now."

"Oh, good—good!" Eleanor handed Tasha an envelope. "Here's some cash. There should be enough for the children to buy gifts for their family and see a movie. Just keep them out of the house until five." She handed her a set of car keys. "Evan's car will be parked in the condominium lot. He thought you might need it."

"Okay . . . but I'm still confused." Tasha studied Eleanor closely. "You seem so different. What's brought on this sudden change of heart?"

Eleanor pursed her lips, looking intently at Tasha. "I guess you could say I've had a revelation of sorts. For the past year I've been angry at God, and my bitterness overflowed onto everyone. Yesterday, little Fiona helped me see myself for what I was—the *bottom mole snowman.*" She actually did smile now. “But I assure you my transformation is genuine.” She grasped Tasha’s hand again. “I owe you an apology. I’m very sorry for the dreadful way I’ve treated you, Tasha. To be honest, I was worried you were taking Evan from me. I hated you for it. I’ve apologized to Evan too, and we both hope you’ll join us for Christmas. I promised Evan I’d do all I can to talk you into it.”

Tasha stared at Eleanor in wonder. Her face looked physically different—younger, brighter, softer. “Thank you. I’d love to come.” She resisted the urge to pinch herself as she told Eleanor goodbye. But a few hours later, as she tugged on her coat, she still felt slightly bamboozled. Was Eleanor’s miraculous transformation real? She patted the envelope and car keys in her coat pocket. No time to question that now. She had three delightful children to take Christmas shopping! Did life get any better than that?

CHAPTER SEVENTEEN

Vera had never experienced such a whirlwind at Christmastime. Everything seemed to change in the days preceding Christmas. It all began shortly after Vera parted company with Bennett and Lola. She'd barely gotten home when Eleanor had shown up with Vera's sewing things. She had been glowing with enthusiasm. Eleanor talked a mile a minute about angel costumes, furniture for the Albrights, plans for a Christmas party at her house, and someone named Murphy.

Vera had difficulty sorting it all out, but Eleanor's enthusiasm proved contagious, so the next day, Vera found herself in the Albrights' condo and, with the help of Evan and his buddy, they arranged a very interesting assortment of fun, youthful, and bright-colored furnishings. By the time all five of the Albrights came home, the place was almost unrecognizable. The children's cries of delight and Kerry's tears of joy made Vera's efforts more than worthwhile.

That same evening was the Christmas pageant at the

church. Fiona had looked sweetly angelic in the beautiful costume Eleanor had loaned to her. Really, it was far more spectacular than anything Vera would've been able to whip up. And to see Eleanor there, as well as Tasha and Evan and Beverly and her husband, well, it felt like Christmas was already complete. Vera felt greedy to hope for anything more.

For the next two days, she occupied herself with her long arm quilting machine. Assisted by Tasha, the quilt's colorful patchwork front was being neatly attached to the moss green fabric for the backing. While supervising the hardworking machine, the two had ample time to talk. It seemed that Tasha, like Vera, was still slightly dumbfounded by Eleanor's amazing transformation. But both of them were happy about it. By now they knew that Eleanor was pulling out all the stops for Christmas.

Tasha had even been invited to decorate the Rasmussen house and, with Evan's help, now claimed the home was picture-perfect. "Honestly," she told Vera, "it could be the cover of a holiday edition of *House Beautiful*. And I didn't take over and try to make it my style. I kept Eleanor in mind the whole time."

Vera had to agree with Tasha as she walked up to the Rasmussen house on Christmas Eve and surveyed the decorations. It was picture-perfect! A light coat of snow had fallen, making the luminaries along the walk shine even more brightly. The house was trimmed with strings of white lights, also reflected in the snow. The windows held electric candles with greens, and the big front window was a burst of glowing color from the enormous Christmas tree shimmering inside.

Vera had barely pressed her finger to the doorbell when she was greeted by Evan. As he took her coat and the oversized box containing the Christmas quilt, Vera paused to admire the foyer, sprung to life with hurricane candles surrounded by luscious greens, as well as numerous poinsettias. Tasha had mentioned they'd borrowed the potted plants from the shop to line the staircase and much more. It even smelled wonderful—a delightful mix of evergreen and spice.

"What do you think?" Tasha asked Vera as she entered from the living room. Her eyes seemed to sparkle even more than the house.

"It's all just perfectly magical!" Vera said. "Just gorgeous."

"Welcome." Eleanor came over to clasp Vera's hand, leading her into the living room where a fire crackled in the fireplace and Christmas music played quietly. The other guests, including the Albright children and Kerry, were happily gathered around the room.

"Your home looks absolutely beautiful," Vera told Eleanor. "So alive and warm."

"It feels good to me too," Eleanor said. "We needed this."

"Merry Christmas," Beverly said to Vera, and her husband, Tom, echoed the greeting before offering to get Vera some eggnog.

"Beverly has provided us with some lovely hors d'oeuvres," Eleanor told Vera. "And I must admit they're delectable." She pointed to a buffet beautifully arranged with platters of tempting appetizers.

"Now I'm glad I skipped lunch," Vera told Beverly.

"She also made a tempting selection of desserts." Eleanor

turned to Beverly. "I should probably admit I was the one who sneaked the sample from your pumpkin pie in the kitchen." She chuckled. "It was amazing."

Beverly exchanged glances with Vera, then laughed heartily. "I finally managed to corrupt Eleanor."

Eleanor's smile was sheepish. "Well, I'll never be a serious sweet eater, but a bit now and then—especially at Christmas—probably won't kill anyone."

They all laughed, then Vera asked Eleanor when they planned to present Kerry with the quilt. "I'm so excited for her to see it."

"But Josh isn't here yet," Tasha said. "Shouldn't we wait for him?"

"Yes, of course." Vera glanced around. "I hadn't noticed. Where is he?"

Tasha shrugged, but Eleanor's expression was slightly coy. "He'll be here soon," Eleanor assured them. "We won't present the quilt until then. In the meantime, we'll just eat, drink, and be merry."

It wasn't long until they heard the sound of male voices coming from the foyer, followed by happy laughter and the stomping of boots. Everyone turned to see who else was here. Vera recognized Josh as he brushed snow out of his hair, but she didn't know the smiling older man with him. Before anyone could say anything, Kerry let out a happy shriek. "Dad!" she cried, rushing toward the gray-haired man. Her children followed, calling out "Grandpa," and everyone else watched in wonder.

"That's Murphy O'Riley," Eleanor whispered to the others. "Kerry's father from Dublin."

Tasha had a knowing smile on her face. "Is that why you went to your travel agent the other—"

"Never mind that." Eleanor shushed Tasha then smiled.

Vera quickly put two and two together. Eleanor must've arranged for Kerry's father to join his family for Christmas. Vera patted her friend on the back. "You're a kind and generous woman, Eleanor Rasmussen."

She waved a hand and brushed away a tear. "Isn't it wonderful to see a family reunited at Christmas?"

Vera nodded, her eyes growing moist too.

"Mr. O'Riley will be our houseguest." Eleanor called out to Evan, "Perhaps you could take his luggage into the blue guest room for me."

Evan came over and kissed his mother on the cheek. "I'm on it, Mom."

Eleanor beamed at him and suddenly the party grew even merrier. Murphy O'Riley went around the room, meeting everyone, shaking hands, and sharing stories of his journey from Dublin. When he shook Vera's hand, his eyes lit up. "Another fine American woman," he said. "I should've come to the States sooner!" He winked at Eleanor. "And you being such a lovely hostess too. How did an old man get so lucky?"

"Is that the blarney talking?" Eleanor teased back.

"No, madam, it is the truth." He pointed to the grand piano. "Does anyone play that?"

Eleanor's smile faded slightly. "My daughter used to play."

"Do you mind if I tickle the keys a bit?"

Eleanor hesitated a moment, then sighed, a smile spreading across her face. "Not at all."

Murphy made himself comfortable at the piano, testing

out the keys and eventually playing "God Rest Ye Merry, Gentlemen." After a few stanzas, several of the guests gathered around to sing along. As Vera joined in the singing, she gazed out over the roomful of guests, realizing that a few weeks ago, these people did not know each other. And yet, here they were, all having a wonderful time together. She watched as Evan took Tasha's hand, leading her over to the doorway to the foyer with a mischievous glint in his eye. He pointed upward to what looked like a small piece of mistletoe hanging overhead. Then he grinned and pulled Tasha close, landing more than just a friendly kiss on her lips. She looked surprised, but not displeased.

Eleanor, standing next to Vera, was watching this little scene too. At first she frowned, but then she let out a small laugh. "Evan hung that mistletoe himself," she said as Murphy began to play "Silver Bells." "Instead of silver bells, I wonder if we'll be hearing wedding bells by next Christmas."

Vera laughed. "Wouldn't that be nice?"

Finally, after much food, singing, laughter, and fun, it was time to present the Christmas quilt to Kerry. Vera wanted Eleanor, as host, to handle the presentation, but Eleanor insisted it was Vera's responsibility. By dinging her fork against her wineglass, she got everyone's attention. "We have something special to do tonight," Eleanor called out. "Please, give your attention to Vera for a moment."

Vera crossed the room to take Fiona's hand. "I want your help, sweetheart, since this was really your idea in the first place." She handed the box containing the quilt to her. "You know what to do with this."

Fiona struggled to hold the heavy box, but carried it over to her mother. "This is for you, Mama."

Kerry tilted her head to one side. "What?"

"Open it," Fiona said, bouncing from one foot to the other.

Kerry lifted the lid and let out a gasp. "Oh my word. It's a patchwork quilt." She lifted it from the box and, standing, held it out fully. "Oh, it's so beautiful. What on earth?" With wide eyes she looked around the room. "What—why—how?"

Vera stepped over, putting an arm around Kerry, who was now crying. "Your sweet Fiona was so worried about you while you were sick, she begged me to make you a patchwork Christmas quilt. But it was too big a task for one person, so I invited my friends to join me—well, they were strangers then, but they're friends now." She waved to Tasha and Eleanor and Beverly, calling them to join her. "And we made this Christmas quilt together." She smiled at her quilting friends. "In the same way this quilt is comprised of different shapes and colors, we four women were different too. We sometimes had our differences, but God has miraculously stitched us together in love." Vera turned back to Kerry. "And you and your family have been stitched into our lives too." She looked out over the group. "May we all be stitched together in love—Merry Christmas, everyone!"

With around 250 books published and 7.5 million sold, **Melody Carlson** is one of the most prolific writers of our times. Writing primarily for women and teens, and in various genres, she has won numerous national awards—including the Rita, Gold Medallion, Carol Award, Christy, and two career achievement awards. Several of her novels have been optioned for film, and her first Hallmark movie, *All Summer Long*, premiered in 2019. Melody makes her home in the Pacific Northwest, where she lives with her husband near the Cascade Mountains. When not writing, Melody enjoys interior design, gardening, camping, and biking.

MEET

Melody

— MelodyCarlson.com —

melodycarlsonauthor

authormelodycarlson

4327